Other books by William Sleator

Novels

Blackbria
House of Sta
Into the Dre

The Green Futures of Tycho
Fingers
Interstellar Pig
Singularity
The Boy Who Reversed Himself
The Duplicate
Strange Attractors
The Spirit House
Others See Us
Dangerous Wishes
The Night the Heads Came
The Beasties
The Boxes
Rewind
Boltzmon!
Marco's Millions
Parasite Pig
The Boy Who Couldn't Die
The Last Universe

Books for Younger Readers

The Angry Moon
Among the Dolls
Once, Said Darlene
That's Silly

Short Story Collection

Oddballs

HELL

WILLIAM

PHONE

SLEATOR

Amulet Books

New York

PUBLISHER'S NOTE: This is a work of fiction. Names, characters, places, and incidents are either the product of the author's imagination or are used fictitiously, and any resemblance to actual persons, living or dead, business establishments, events, or locales is entirely coincidental.

Library of Congress Cataloging-in-Publication Data:
Sleator, William.
Hell phone / by William Sleator.
p. cm.
Summary: Seventeen-year-old Nick buys a used cell phone only to call his girlfriend, but strange and desperate people keep calling—one of them a denizen of hell—begging for or demanding his help.
ISBN-13: 978-0-8109-5479-3
ISBN-10: 0-8109-5479-6
[1. Cellular telephones—Fiction. 2. Supernatural—Fiction. 3. Hell—Fiction. 4. Future life—Fiction.] I. Title.
PZ7.S6313Hel 2006
[Fic]—dc22
2006009001

Designer: Chad W. Beckerman
Production Manager: Alexis Mentor

Published in 2006 by Amulet Books,
an imprint of Harry N. Abrams, Inc.

Printed and bound in U.S.A.
1 3 5 7 9 10 8 6 4 2

HNA
harry n. abrams, inc.
a subsidiary of La Martinière Groupe
115 West 18th Street
New York, NY 10011
www.amuletbooks.com

This book is for Stephen Weiner, who has helped me so much with many of my books—and given me great titles for them, too.

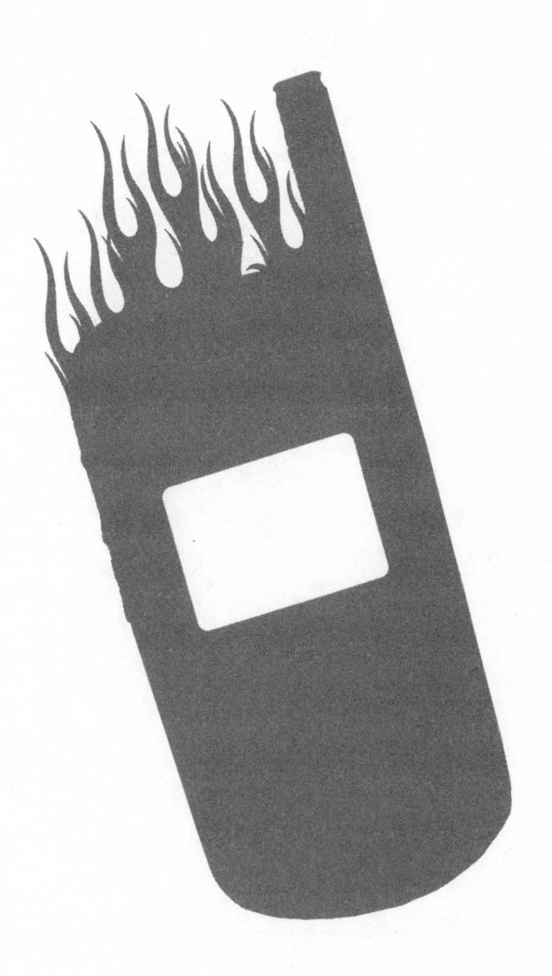

1

I didn't have much time to buy the phone because school gets out at three and the only discount store that sold phones, all the way across town, closed at five, and I had to be at work by five-thirty. But if I rode fast on my bike—not a car, like a lot of the other kids at school had, but an old bike—I might be able to make it, if it didn't take too long to pick out the phone.

"I'm getting a surprise for us today," I told Jen as we left the building—when she wasn't at practice we spent the time between school and my job together. "So I have to hurry now."

"What surprise?" she asked, grinning at me. She was a sophomore and I was a junior. She was the star of the girls' soccer team and had long red hair and a great body. A lot of guys were always after her but it was me she liked. I could hardly believe it. She had practice today, so getting the phone wouldn't interfere with our time together.

"You'll find out the surprise tonight," I said, teasing her.

She looked puzzled. "But you know we can't see each other tonight."

"You'll find out tonight," I said again. We had reached the bike rack. I unlocked my bike, dropped my books in the basket, and kissed her quickly. "Talk to you later." I put on my helmet, and rode off at top speed.

Luckily the weather was good—a bright spring day, not too hot. I rode fast but also kept my eyes on the traffic. No accidents now! I had finally saved up some money to buy a used cell phone and pay for a certain number of minutes—it all depended on what the store offered. And after I earned more money I could pay for more time. Now Jen and I would be able to talk every night.

It took a while to find the phone store, which was in a crummy neighborhood, and I didn't get there until four. But it was a good feeling, sort of like an adventure, and most of my life—except Jen—was so routine. I loved this non-routine feeling of adventure!

I parked and carefully double-locked the bike and ran in.

The dusty glass cabinet was full of phones, some really outdated looking, some small and sleek. The fat man behind the counter had a cigarette in his mouth. He put down the music magazine he was reading—the cover story was about Megadeth—and looked at me without getting up. "Yeah?" he said around the cigarette. He didn't seem too interested. I'm seventeen and don't have the money for expensive-looking clothes—I was wearing old, threadbare jeans and a T-shirt.

"I got a flier in the mail that says you have the cheapest phones in town. What kind of phone have you got for . . . er . . . twenty bucks?" I asked him, a little afraid of his reaction. "And how many minutes for thirty bucks more?"

He took the cigarette out of his mouth, blew out reeking smoke, and grinned at me. "Not a whole hell of a lot," he said.

"Well, that's what I've got," I said. "And I'm kind of in a hurry."

"For that price I got only one," he said. "Take it or leave it." He unlocked the case and, to my surprise, took out one of the newer-looking ones, a nice shining silver color. It was small, and had a good-sized display and five function keys above the numbers. "For thirty bucks you get a hundred and fifty minutes."

I loved the phone, but I had to ask. "Why is that the cheapest? Some of those older, bigger ones look like they might be cheaper."

"It's used," he said. "Previous owner brought it back and we refurbished it. Except I couldn't get the caller ID to work. It's been disabled." He shrugged. "Don't know why, don't know how, and it couldn't be fixed, but there it is. Most people like to know who's calling them before they answer. On this phone, you can't know. That's why it's cheap."

That didn't seem so bad to me. The whole reason I was getting the phone was to talk to Jen. Mom had trouble making the regular monthly payments on our phone at home, so the phone company was always shutting off our service. And anyway, when the phone was working Mom hated it when I made "frivolous" calls. There was no extension, the phone was in the living room, where Mom watched TV after work, so I couldn't make personal calls on it when she was home, even if she would have let me. There was no privacy in the trailer where we lived. But I was used to waiting to talk to my other friends at school and making plans there. Talking to Jen in the evening was what really mattered. That's what this phone was for. She was the only person I was going to talk to on it. So who else was going to call me? I didn't need caller ID. And I didn't have the time or the money to be choosy. "I'll take it," I said.

"No returns," the fat man said. "I've learned my lesson."

"Fine," I said, in a hurry. Why would I want to return it?

"And you can't change the number."

"Fine," I said again, impatient.

The fat man put the cigarette back in his mouth, made me sign an agreement and fill out a form, and then put copies of the form and the agreement, and the phone and the charger in a plastic bag, and held out his other hand. I handed him the money and took the bag and was out of there. The man told me the phone was already charged, because he'd been working on it, but I didn't even take the time to turn it on and check it out. I was in a hurry, and anyway the place was rank with the stink of his cigarette—some weird brand I guessed. It smelled like rotten eggs.

I worked the evening shift in the staff cafeteria of a hospital not far from school. It didn't pay much, but it fit my schedule—working five-thirty to eight-thirty gave me time to be with Jen after school when she didn't have practice and also get my homework done later. I got there just on time. Of course I couldn't use the phone at work, either. I put it in the locker where I kept my apron and gloves and stuff.

I didn't mind dishing out the food to nurses and doctors and nurse's aides and orderlies, though some of them had complained at first about my long hair getting in the food—it was dark blond and kinky and fell to my shoulders—so I had to wear a hairnet, which was sort of embarrassing. But Jen loved my hair and I wasn't going to cut it.

The worst thing about the job was the twenty-gallon milk machine. Taking out the empty cylinder was nothing, but it was tricky getting the heavy full one off the dolly, and one time I had spilled it, twenty gallons of milk all over the floor behind the counter. Bridget, the loud-mouthed boss, had almost fired me then, so now I was nervous every time I had to change it. But I hadn't spilled it again, and I didn't spill it that night. I just wanted work to be over so I could call Jen and surprise her. So of course it went on forever.

But finally eight-thirty rolled around. I would have liked to call her immediately from the hospital but it was too noisy, and so was the busy street. I knew I could get home before nine and that wasn't too late.

Mom wasn't home—she had a second job most nights, waitressing. I locked up my bike, dropped my books on my small, bare desk—no computer for me—and was about to call Jen. I wasn't sure exactly how to turn on the phone, and fumbled impatiently with it for a few seconds. I wanted to talk to Jen!

And then I found the right button.

The phone rang the instant I turned it on, and I almost dropped it. You could probably choose the ring, but I hadn't done that yet. This one sounded like a crying cat, meowing in pain or hunger. It was really irritating.

Of course there was no name on the display, it was just blinking. The caller ID had been disabled. It *was* a little scary. I gulped, and told myself it was only a friend of the previous owner who didn't know the phone had been returned and sold to someone else. I just had to tell whoever it was that I wasn't who she or he thought, so this person wouldn't call me again, and then I could call Jen.

I hesitated, and the phone mewed at me again. I jumped. Then I pressed the green talk button.

"Hello," I said, tentatively. "Er, listen, I think—"

"Oh, I see," a cool male voice interrupted me. "So the dope thought he could double-cross me. He sold it and ran away. He's toast now," he added calmly.

My heart was pounding. The voice sounded really icy. "Well, er, now I own this phone, so I guess, er, you'll have to stop—"

"So it's going to have to be you now, whoever you are," the suave voice interrupted me again. Then he became businesslike. "What's your name? What's your address? *Where are you right now?*"

2

I hung up, then immediately dialed Jen's number so that the maniac couldn't call me back. My hand was shaking. I had no idea what was going on.

Her mother answered, of course. "Hello, Mrs. Golding. This is Nick," I said, trying to sound normal. "Is Jen there?"

"Why, Nick," she said. "What a surprise." I knew she didn't really approve of me, because of my being poor and having no father. But she also knew I was an okay guy, and hardworking, so she hadn't tried to interfere—yet.

"Yeah. I saved up the money from work to buy this phone," I said. Scared as I was by the guy who had called me, I still knew what to say to Jen's mother.

There was a beep on the phone. That guy was trying to call me again!

"Sounds like someone's calling you," Jen's mother said.

"That's okay. I don't need to answer," I said. "I just would like to talk to Jen, please."

"Hold on," she said.

The phone kept beeping. The guy wasn't giving up. I'd turn the thing off as soon as I finished talking to Jen.

"Nick?" Jen said. "You bought a cell phone?"

Her mother had ruined the surprise. "Yeah. I saved up the money. So we could talk at night."

"That's *great*," she said. The phone beeped again. "Sounds like somebody's trying to call you," she said. "Did you give somebody else the number?"

"No, no," I said. I hadn't wanted to get into this with her, but what else could I say? "It's a used phone—that's why I could afford it. Somebody who knew the first owner called this number the second I turned it on. I told him I was somebody else, but he kept talking so I hung up. I just want him to stop, so I'm not going to answer, and then maybe he'll give up. I bought it to talk to you. Only to talk to you. That's what the minutes are for."

"Well, if that guy keeps bothering you, you should report his number to the phone company," she said.

"Yeah, except this phone has no caller ID. That's why it was cheap. So I don't know his number. I . . . I can't know who's calling me."

"Oh," she said. She sounded funny. *I* probably sounded funny. "I never heard of a cell phone without caller ID."

"Yeah, well, I bought it from a weird place that sent me a flier." This conversation was not going at all the way I had imagined it. "This was the surprise I was talking about."

The phone beeped again. "Oh," she said again, not sounding happy or surprised.

"Listen, this person will have to give up if I keep not answering," I told her, hoping I was right. "I'll give you the number, but maybe you shouldn't call until he stops calling me. After that, I'll know it's you and not him. I won't give the number to anybody else."

"But what if other people call you?" she asked. "Other people probably have this number. It's kind of creepy, having somebody else's phone without caller ID. Maybe you should just return it and get a different one. Or change the number of the phone."

"The store doesn't let you return them. And I can't change the number. That's the other reason it was cheap. And I already paid for a hundred and fifty minutes on this number, before I knew this guy would call me. I'm stuck with it for that long. Just let me give you the number." I got the documentation out of the bag from the store and told her. "But don't call until I tell you it's okay."

"You sound . . . different," she said, as the phone beeped again.

Should I tell her what the guy had said? I didn't want to make her worry. But I needed to tell somebody, and who else was there? Mom sure wouldn't be sympathetic about it. She'd think I'd done something stupid. "Well, you're right, it *is* creepy," I said. "When I told the guy who called that I wasn't who he thought, he said the other owner had double-crossed him and that now he was toast. And then he wanted to know where I lived."

"You didn't tell him, did you?" she said, sounding shocked.

"No, no, of course I didn't! I'm not *that* stupid. But it sure sounded like he was planning to call again. Like he wanted me to *do* something. I just don't want to talk to him at all. I'm going to keep this thing turned off except for when I call you."

The phone beeped. "I think that's a good idea," she

said. "Whoever is trying to call you seems pretty persistent. Maybe we better hang up and you can turn it off now, right away, so he'll get the message."

"Okay," I said, feeling crestfallen. "Sorry. I'm sure this will stop and everything will be fine. I was just . . . trying to find a way to talk to you more."

"I know you were, Nick," she said, sounding more like her usual self. "I'll see you at school tomorrow."

"Okay. Bye," I said, and we hung up.

The phone mewed.

I had said I would turn it off, but now I didn't want to. Now I was angry. This guy had ruined my first conversation with Jen on the new phone—the phone I bought with money I earned from work. I wanted to make him stop calling, period. I answered. "Listen," I said, without waiting for him to say anything. "Stop calling me. Now. I paid good money for this phone and it wasn't so I could talk to you."

The woman on the other end burst into tears. "Trang?" she cried. "You're not Trang! What happened to him?" Now she was openly sobbing. "What am I going to do without Trang? Who will save me?"

I had no idea what was going on. "Trang?" I said. "I never heard of Trang. Is he the one who used to own this phone?"

"Oh, what am I going to do?" the woman wailed. "Where is he? Where is he? I'm so afraid!"

"Who are you?" I asked. "What's wrong?"

"Are you sure Trang's not there? I need him so much! What am I going to do without him? This was the only way I could reach him. Oh, dear God!"

"Please," I tried again. "If you could just—"

"Oh, I've got to find him. I've got to—"

Suddenly she hung up.

I set the phone down on my little desk and stared at it. This beautiful thin silver phone, that made a bell-like sound when you folded it up. It had been something I had wanted for so long.

And now all it meant was trouble.

This was a perfect time to talk to Jen about anything we wanted. But now I was almost afraid to turn the phone on. I'd turned it off so I could think. I wondered if I should call the police. If that woman wasn't completely delusional, she sounded like she was in real trouble. But what did I have to say to the cops? I had nothing to go on.

What had I gotten myself into?

In our tiny, greasy kitchen—Mom worked so much she never had the time or energy to really clean it—I boiled some water and poured it over a package of dried noodles I dumped in a bowl. I knew I should be eating salad or vegetables or something like that, but we didn't have any, and when we did they were always wilted and old. I ate all the fruit and vegetables

I could during school lunch, though there wasn't much there, and at the hospital cafeteria they let me take leftovers at the end of my shift.

I was usually hungry all the time but now I wasn't, because of the problems with the phone. I slurped down the noodles, hardly tasting them.

I remembered to hide the phone in my backpack before Mom came home. She was usually tired and grouchy when she worked evenings, and of course she'd think the phone was a waste of money. I sat at my desk and painstakingly wrote out my homework by hand. It took a long time because I had to make it as legible as possible—everybody else had computers and I knew the teachers preferred papers that were printed and not handwritten. But I had to get good grades anyway because I had to get a scholarship or else I wouldn't be able to go to college—and if I didn't go to college I'd always be as poor as Mom and I were now.

At least tomorrow was Friday. That meant Jen and I could go out after work. I would hardly have any money to spend, because of the phone, but Jen had always been good about that, and she'd help me out until I got my check in a week.

I had trouble concentrating. What was the story

behind the phone? Who was Trang? He seemed to be the previous owner of the phone, who had been the one to disable the caller ID for some reason I couldn't understand. If I found Trang, he might be able to explain what was going on and who the terrified woman was. But it would be very hard to find him.

Would the guy at the discount store tell me who had returned the phone to him? I kind of doubted it. He seemed like a jerk.

I heard the sound of the key in the door—you could hear everything in this trailer—and Mom dropping her purse on the chair next to the door and her footsteps going into the kitchen. I could tell by her footsteps that she was more tired than usual tonight. That wasn't good. I was lucky tomorrow was Friday, and I could stay away for the evening, with Jen. What would I do without Jen?

"Nick!" Mom called out, and I realized I had forgotten to clean up after eating the noodles—I preferred to eat them in a bowl rather than in the plastic cup they came in. Mom didn't keep the kitchen very clean, but she still refused to clean up after me.

I jumped up and hurried over to the kitchen, which was a sink and stove and a couple of small cabinets along one side of the tiny living room. Mom just looked at me, slumping, her face sagging. "Sit down, Mom. I'll wash out that bowl. Can I get you anything?"

She managed to smile at me. That was a relief. "I'm lucky you're a good boy, Nick. What would I do if you were a troublemaker? That's all I'd need." She briefly stroked my hair. Then she sank into her old easy chair, with the threadbare arms—that chair and the TV filled up the whole living room—and picked up the remote. "A cup of tea would be wonderful," she said, and turned on the TV. At least I wasn't going to have problems with her tonight.

I kept the phone turned off the next day; Jen and I had the same lunch period and always met at the same place. "You look tired, Nick," she said, when we sat down.

I loved it that she was worried about me. I took a bite of pizza. I knew it was junk food, but that's what the school cafeteria had today. At least I had gotten a salad and an apple. "It's that phone. It worries me. I'm afraid to turn it on because some nut will call me up."

"Somebody else called you?"

I told her about the woman. Now she looked more worried. She shook her head. "Should we call the police?"

I shrugged. "What would I tell them? They'll just

think I'm some crazy kid." I'd learned that long-haired guys were not at the top of the police department's "most trustworthy" list. I often got weird looks from cops when I was just riding around town; I knew they wouldn't pay any attention to this story. "If I could find this Trang person who used to own the phone, maybe I could get some answers. But I can't get any numbers from this phone. He's obviously afraid of the first guy who called me, who said he was toast. I'm . . . I'm kind of afraid of him, too."

She leaned forward and smiled—when Jen smiled her whole lovely face lit up. "Don't worry. There's nothing he can do to you if we don't let him. We'll figure something out." She thought for a moment, her head to the side. "When you pick me up tonight, why don't you show the phone to Dad? He knows about stuff like that. Maybe he could help."

I liked Jen's father better than her mother. Even though he was a businessman, and made a lot of money, I didn't get the feeling that he disapproved of me because I was poor, the way her mother did. He asked me about my life and seemed to approve of the way I did well in school and worked so hard. I kind of got the feeling he believed I would make something of myself. I had never thought of asking him to help me with anything. I felt a certain reluctance about showing him the phone. What would happen if *he* talked to one of those people?

But it might be a help to show it to someone with authority, and I knew I couldn't tell Mom about it. Jen was right about me being tired. I hadn't slept well, worrying about the phone.

I did make it through school okay. And after school, before work, Jen and I sat together in the park, near the sparkling fountain. It was another beautiful day, and we talked and laughed together about stuff, and held hands, and kissed occasionally. I began to relax, and almost forgot about the phone.

I was glad of the uniform at work, in case I spilled anything—I didn't want to look like a mess in front of Jen's folks. It went on forever, as usual, but at last it was over. I rode my bike through the quiet streets of Jen's nice neighborhood, and felt almost confident. Was there a chance that her father might be able to help? It was hard to believe, but I refused to give up hope. I told myself I'd get rid of those crazy people, even if I needed a parent to help me, like a little kid, and get the phone working right. And then everything would be better than before.

As usual, I went around to the back of Jen's house

and locked the bike to the steps that led to the back porch, and took a brief look at the yard, lush with flowers—her mother was big on gardening. Then I went back around and rang the front doorbell.

Jen opened the front door immediately and kissed me fast, before her parents could see. Then we went into the living room, which seemed so fancy to me, but which all of them just accepted as normal. Since it was after eight-thirty, her parents had already eaten and were having coffee. We all greeted each other politely. They were probably the same age as my mother, but looked younger. They didn't have to work as hard, and could afford cosmetic procedures.

"So, Jen says you're having some problems with a cell phone," her father said, after Jen and I had sat down—not on the same couch.

"Did she tell you what's going on?" I asked him. He had taken off his suit jacket but was still wearing a white shirt and tie. The skin on his face was very tight.

"A little. But I'd like to hear it all from you."

I told him about the threatening guy. I toned down the sobbing woman, making it sound like she was just worried about finding her boyfriend. If he thought her life might be in danger he really would make me call the cops. Now I felt a little uneasy about telling him anything, as a matter of fact, but it was too late to stop. As I talked, he looked more and more puzzled—and a little worried, too.

"What does your mother say about all this?" he asked me when I finished.

"I didn't tell her. She'd think it was a waste of money to buy the phone. And even if she didn't, I don't want to worry her. She works so hard. She has enough on her mind."

I glanced for a second at Jen's mother and saw the merest flicker of disapproval. She probably thought Mom should be married to somebody who had a good job, instead of working herself and raising me alone. She didn't understand that some people don't have that kind of luck.

"Can I have a look at this phone?" Jen's father said.

I got it out of my backpack and handed it over to him, strangely reluctant to let somebody else touch it. "Remember, as soon as you turn it on it will probably ring, and there'll be some nut on the phone—either the threatening guy, or the woman who cries all the time."

He looked it over without turning it on. "A nice one. How much did you say you paid for it?"

"Twenty. And thirty for a hundred and fifty minutes."

He smiled ironically. "At that price, it's not surprising it has some glitches." He hesitated. Then he pressed the button to turn it on.

To my surprise, it did not ring immediately. He glanced at me, then back to the phone. He pushed some buttons. Then he looked startled—and not pleased. "Did you ever get a chance to fool around with it before it started ringing?" he asked me.

"No. Every time I turned it on, it rang immediately, and the calls were so weird I just stopped turning it on at all."

"Uh . . . maybe you should look at this, Nick. But not you, Jen," he added quickly.

I went over to his chair and leaned over and looked at the display. Fires flickered on it. The words GAMES FROM REAL HELL in creepy black gothic letters scrolled across the screen over and over again.

Again, as when I had gone to buy the phone, I had that feeling of excitement, of something out of the ordinary happening. I was also a little surprised by the possessiveness I felt for the troublesome thing. "Gee, I never had a chance to see that, or look at those games, or anything," I said. "Every time I turned it on it—"

The display went blank and the phone emitted its irritating whining-cat ring. Everybody but me jerked at the sound. I seemed to have gotten used to it.

It rang again. Jen's father seemed momentarily confused. Then he pressed the green button and put it to his ear. I stood there worrying as he sat there listening. Which one had called him? Or was it someone new?

"Wait. Hold on a second. This isn't my phone. You need to talk to the guy who bought it." He handed it to me with a puzzled expression.

"Hello? Hello?" said an entirely new male voice. "You buy phone?"

"Yeah, I'm the one who bought it."

"Be careful. That all I can say. Do not talk to them. Do not do what they say."

The guy had a heavy accent. "Are you Trang?" I asked him, feeling strangely thrilled to hear from him. "Where are you? Can we talk?"

"I am very sorry. Not good idea for me to return it. Now you have problem." And I wondered: Was the threatening guy really going to be *my* problem now? "You must throw away phone," Trang continued. "Very dangerous."

"Wait! Can't you explain why—"

He hung up.

I gulped, then quickly turned it off.

"Who was that?" said Jen.

"What did he say?" her father asked.

"I think it was Trang, the previous owner, the one who disabled the caller ID." I actually felt out of breath.

"And?" her father pressed me.

"He told me not to listen to the others, not to do what they say." I didn't say he said I should throw it away. Then Jen's father would agree. He'd probably want me to throw it away anyway. It *had* been a mistake to show it to him after all. Because as much as it scared me, I was suddenly not sure I wanted to throw it away. At least not yet. I wanted to see what **GAMES FROM REAL HELL** was all about.

"I don't like this," Jen's father said. "You should get rid of it."

My heart sank. If I hadn't been so tired I would have known better than to show it to him. If I argued with him he might not like me as much, and that would be a big problem. And still I said, "But I spent all that money on it."

He shrugged. "Not so much."

"But I worked hard for that money. I can't just throw it away and have nothing for it."

He paused. I hoped he wasn't going to offer to lend me the money for another phone. I could borrow money from Jen, but not from her father.

"I think you should do what George says," Jen's mother said. "He knows what he's talking about."

"But that guy who just called, Trang, *he* sounded okay," I said. "If I could just find him, get in touch with him somehow, he could explain everything. And I'd still have a phone." I paused. "He didn't sound weird when he talked to you, did he?" I asked Jen's father.

"No. But he was warning you about the phone."

Why had I opened my big mouth? Why had I told them *anything* Trang had said? I should never have showed it to them at all.

"If it's dangerous, I don't want Jen to have anything to do with it," her mother said. "And if you have it, then she has something to do with it."

Were they going to try to keep Jen away from me because of this phone? Then it *really* wasn't worth it. As curious as I was about the phone, Jen was a million times more important—the most important part of my life.

I had an idea.

"Okay," I said. "I know what to do. Could I use your phone for a minute, please?"

"Sure," Jen's father said.

I went over to the table where the phone was and called directory assistance. When they answered, I asked for the city sanitation department, and wrote down the number on the pad next to the phone—everything was well-organized in this house. I knew they'd be closed now, but there would be a message. All the message said was that they were closed and when they would be open, but I listened longer than that before I hung up. Then I turned back to Jen's father.

"You know, there's toxic stuff in phones like this," I said. "They're like computers. You can't just throw them in the trash—that would be polluting. But the sanitation department will be open on Monday and I'll take it there, and they'll take the right measures, and be sure it doesn't cause any problems." I paused, hoping they would believe the next part. "And I won't use it again before I give it to them. I swear it." Her parents looked at each other. I could tell her mother was waiting for her father's reaction.

He nodded. "That's very responsible of you, Nick," he said. "A lot of people your age wouldn't think that way about it. I think that's an excellent idea. Do it as soon as possible. And maybe—well, we'll see."

Was he going to offer to get me another phone? I probably shouldn't accept it if he did.

Her father looked at his watch. "And now they better go get something to eat."

And in a few minutes Jen was pulling their second, smaller car out of the driveway. "So what are you going to do about the phone?" she asked me, before turning onto the street.

"I don't know," I said. I waited a beat. "But I might not throw it away on Monday. And your parents don't have to know that."

She looked at me without any expression for a moment. "You mean you lied?"

I shook my head. "I'm not throwing it away yet," I said again.

I watched her. A mixture of emotions played across her face. I knew she didn't like the phone. I also knew she felt her mother was too strict, and that she didn't in the least mind disobeying her. Her mouth began to form a smile at the trick we were playing.

Then the smile faded. "But you lied. I never knew you to lie before. It's that phone that made you lie."

We were just sitting there at the end of the driveway. I didn't want her parents to notice. "Let's go to Joe's," I said. It was an inexpensive place where we often got something to eat. "We can talk about it."

She sighed, but she pulled out of the driveway and

turned in the direction of Joe's. Now I was excited. It was a nervous, anxious kind of excitement—that I was involved in something adult and important that maybe I couldn't or shouldn't try to handle. It felt like a game, too, and not just because of those games Jen's dad had found. I could turn the phone on and off and control the interaction. And I could always give the phone to the police, if I had to. But for now, it was mine, and I wanted to find out more. "I feel like I'm meant to have this phone, Jen," I said. "Like I'm supposed to do something to figure out what's going on with that woman and Trang. And it had weird games on it, games I've never seen on a computer—that's what your father didn't want you to see. Who knows what else it has?"

"But what about that other guy? The threatening one? That worries me, Nick."

"I can ignore him," I said. And then it came pouring out. "Look, I spend my whole life being a good boy, working every day after school, doing all my homework without a computer, getting good grades anyway, always being so nice to my mother, even when she's in a lousy mood. Just once, *once in my life*, I'd like to do something interesting, maybe even dangerous. Don't you think I can handle it? It's not like

I'm driving drunk or doing drugs. I'm trying to help someone. Solve a mystery."

I had never said anything like this before. She looked at me, then back to the road. I waited impatiently for her reaction.

And then she smiled at me, conspiratorially this time. "Maybe you've got a point there," she said, before turning back to the road. "Just don't get hurt. And I don't want to get hurt either. If it seems dangerous I'll *make* you turn it in or throw it away. But in the meantime—let's see what it can do."

I wanted to hug her. And soon I would.

4

A lot of kids hung out at Joe's. Not the rich kids, who had their own clique, and fancy clothes and fancy cars, and their own hangouts. Regular kids came here, kids without a lot of money—though they all had more money than I did.

But I bet none of them had a phone with **GAMES FROM REAL HELL** on it. Now the phone was making me feel important. Should I show it to anybody else?

But the whole reason I had bought the phone was to talk to Jen, and only to Jen. I felt a pang of guilt. The phone was turning into something different than I had planned. *Had* it changed me already, as Jen had wondered?

Jen had to be home by ten-thirty, an early curfew it seemed to us, and we had wasted a lot of time stupidly showing the phone to her parents, which we never should have done. It didn't matter what time *I* got home because Mom worked late on weekends.

We found a booth and sat down. It didn't seem like any of our friends were here tonight. I felt slightly disappointed. Then I realized that was stupid. Even if I *were* going to show the phone to anybody else, it was still too early to do that. I had to learn more about how it worked first.

I usually got a salad here, because I knew it was healthy. But I had decided not to be such a good boy all the time anymore. I could get something else for once. Jen ordered a chicken Caesar salad. I ordered a double cheeseburger with fries. Then I got the phone out of my backpack.

"Do you have to fool around with that thing *now?*" Jen said.

"Just for a second," I said. "Just until the food comes." I patted the bench next to me. "Sit over here so you can see, too—and so I can be next to you."

She smiled and sat down beside me. That was one of the good things about Jen. She forgave easily and was a good sport.

I turned on the phone. It didn't ring immediately.

That was good. I wanted to check out the games before talking to any of the callers. I fooled around with the buttons, trying to find GAMES FROM REAL HELL again. What had her father done to find it? For a second I wished I had asked him. Then I knew that would have been a mistake.

So I just randomly pressed the buttons for awhile, and finally I found GAMES. "Look at this," I said to Jen, searching through them. And then there it was, the flames, and GAMES FROM REAL HELL.

She looked a little surprised, and not necessarily pleased.

"Cool, right?" I asked her.

"It depends," she said.

I pressed SELECT, and a list appeared above the flames. TORTURE MASTER, ATTEMPTS TO ESCAPE, JOYFUL SINS TO GET YOU IN were just a few of them.

"Could you try something else?" Jen asked me. "It looks like these will take my appetite away."

"Sure, sure," I said, and pressed EXIT.

I could look at the games later. I pressed more buttons. The phone didn't seem to do that much after all. There were no other games. All I could find was a list of songs you could download and play. Neither of us had heard of any of them, and most of them were in an entirely different language from English. "That must be music Trang liked."

"Looks Vietnamese," Jen said. Two of her friends from soccer were Vietnamese sisters, Thu and Chau, so she probably knew what she was talking about.

There was already music blaring in the restaurant, so I didn't try to play any songs. I started to press more combinations of buttons, finding nothing. This phone was more limited than all the other phones I had seen. All it had was songs and games—it couldn't do text messages or e-mail or take pictures or anything else, and it had no caller ID. No wonder it had been cheap.

The wailing cat mewed.

"I'm going to have to change that, somehow," I said. "It's really irritating."

It mewed again.

"That's for sure," Jen said.

"Should I answer it?"

"I thought we came here to be together," she said.

I looked at her as the phone mewed again. She sounded almost petulant. She had never sounded like that before. I felt another pang. What was I doing, anyway, fooling with this phone when Jen and I had our precious time together? I turned off the phone and put it in my backpack. When I was alone, I could find out if it could do anything else.

Then our food came. It had been a long time since I'd had a double cheeseburger and fries. It would have tasted better if Jen had been in a better mood. But for the first time, conversation seemed to have dried up between us.

"I'm sorry, Jen," I said. "I already told you, the only reason I bought the phone was to call you. I never thought it would turn out like this."

She didn't answer me until she finished chewing a piece of chicken. Then she said, "In that case, maybe you really should get rid of it, and save up your money again and get another one."

"Aren't you even curious? I mean about what's going on with these people who are calling me? What they want? What their story is?"

"Don't you think we have enough going on in our own lives without getting involved with weird people who sound dangerous?" she snapped at me.

My heart sank. This was the closest we had ever come to a fight. All because of the phone, which I had bought to bring us closer.

But I couldn't lie to her. I couldn't tell her I was going to throw it away. Lying to her parents was one thing, but lying to Jen was entirely different.

"Here's what I promise," I said. "I won't use it when I'm with you. Never again. When I'm with you, it's just us. Like before."

"That's a promise?" she said, softening.

I took her hand. "A promise," I said.

She smiled, like her old self, and squeezed my hand. "I believe you," she said. Then she took her hand away. But before she had another bite of her salad she said, "I understand what you said about always being a good boy, always doing the right thing, and wanting some risk and adventure for a change. Okay, fine. For a little while. But the real truth is, I'll feel better when you get it out of your system and get rid of that thing—and those people calling you."

"Nothing will happen to me," I said, trying to sound as sincere as possible.

But how could I know that?

Some kids we knew showed up, and we hung out with them for awhile. But I kept surreptitiously looking at my watch. I wanted some time alone in the car with Jen before ten-thirty.

But the other kids kept talking, and it turned out

we had only fifteen minutes. It was nice, it was always nice. But I didn't feel quite the same closeness we had always felt before. The phone really had come between us. Was I going to have to make a choice?

Before we got out of the car at her house, where my bike was, I said, "Listen, Jen. I'll keep the phone for the weekend. I'll see what happens in the next two days. I'll be totally honest with you about everything. And if we decide it's wrong to keep the phone, I'll take it to the police. A promise."

She kissed me again. And this time it was like before.

I rode home fast, eager to explore the phone some more. I got home before eleven. Mom wouldn't be back until two. This was a good opportunity since I couldn't use the phone when she was home—she'd hear it ring, she'd hear me talking, she'd hear everything in this place.

But as soon as I turned it on, it mewed. Who would it be? The creepy guy, the crying woman, or Trang? I hoped it would be Trang, but I doubted it.

"Why didn't you answer me before?" the creepy guy wanted to know. "It's not easy for me to get through. You're supposed to answer when I call."

I actually started to tell him I was with my girlfriend,

but stopped myself in time: The less he knew about me, and especially Jen, the better. I was scared, but I tried to sound cool. "You know I can't tell who's calling me on this thing," I told him. "Caller ID's disabled. Do you know why Trang did that?"

"Trang?" he said, sounding very suspicious. "How do *you* know about Trang?"

Mistake. I shouldn't have given away what I knew—and I especially shouldn't let him know that the woman or Trang had called me. But in a second it was obvious what to tell him. "When he returned the phone he was in a hurry. He didn't bother to delete everything. I was able to find out that he was the previous owner. And I'm guessing the previous owner had to be the one to doctor the phone."

"Hmm. So you're not as dumb as you sound," he said. "Maybe you'll be more useful than I thought. Maybe you *can* get me to where Lola is."

"Who's Lola?" I said, though I was pretty sure it was the woman who cried so much.

"You don't need to know that—not yet, anyway. Forget I mentioned her. Now listen, there's some stuff you need to buy, to finish what Trang started before he chickened out. You go to an electronics store and you get—"

"Wait a minute," I said. "You don't understand. I bought this phone because it only cost twenty bucks. I blew all my extra money. I go to school and I work. I don't have the money to go out and buy expensive electronic equipment."

"Listen, kid, I'm in a hurry. The situation is getting more desperate every minute. I don't care how poor you are. You're going to go and get what I need, and you're going to do it immediately, even if you have to steal it. I need a flash, and I need a special computer battery pack. You got a pencil? You better write this down so you get it right."

I found myself scrambling for a pencil and a piece of paper, not really knowing why, since I had no intention of helping this creep. But I scribbled down the information anyway. "And after you get it, I'll tell you how to hook it up to the phone."

"What's the stuff for?" I dared to ask.

"Maybe I'll tell you, if you do what I want. That'll be your reward. Get that stuff *now.*" And he hung up.

There was no way I could get that stuff, it was completely impossible. And what could he do to me if I didn't? He was just a voice on the phone, I told myself.

But I was still scared. I actually started trying to think of possible ways to get what he wanted.

• • •

"Stop it!" I said out loud. I needed to distract myself. It wasn't even midnight yet. I had plenty of time—on Saturdays I worked the lunch shift at the hospital so I didn't have to get up as early as for school.

I went right to **GAMES FROM REAL HELL**. I selected **ATTEMPTS TO ESCAPE.**

There were several different ways. I didn't read them all, I just went to the first one, **DON'T LOOK BACK.**

The display showed a dark ascending tunnel, and at the very end, far, far away and high above, was a blue light, like the sky. I pressed a few keys until I figured out how to move forward, and also backward. It was the big middle key, which had a line on each of the four sides; the top one was forward, the bottom one was backward. Naturally I chose to move forward. I pressed the key repeatedly. It went very slowly. The sky hardly got any closer at all.

And then, out of nowhere, a luscious looking birthday cake, covered with swirls of chocolate icing, came swooping down from above, and quickly disappeared behind me. Just seeing it gave me hunger pangs. Without thinking, I moved backward to get a better look at it.

Flames engulfed the display. They looked so blazing hot I could practically feel it. **GAME OVER** appeared in black gothic letters.

Now I got it. It was like the ancient Greek myth of Orpheus. He's the greatest musician in the world, and plays an instrument called a lyre. With his music he can charm anything—gods, wild animals, even stones. His beautiful wife, Eurydice, dies and goes to the underworld. He goes down to bring her up to the living again and charms all the guardians with his music. But she can only follow him out if he doesn't look back at her. And he does look behind, and she has to go back, and Orpheus can never get Eurydice out again. In order to win this game, I had to avoid all temptations to turn around and look back.

I started over again. Soon enough, the cake came gliding down. This time I ignored it and kept going. Then came a huge, glittering diamond that riveted the eye. It was tempting, but I managed to fight the impulse to look back at it—jewels didn't interest me anyway. The patch of blue sky got significantly closer. I began to think I could win this game.

Then came an incredibly hot woman, like the sexiest of movie stars, taking her clothes off. Without thinking I stepped back to get a better look at her.

Flames engulfed the screen again. **GAME OVER.**

I was determined to get out of here; there was something addictive about this game. I started over again. This time I was able to ignore the cake, the diamond, even the hot woman.

And then Jen's face came floating down.

"Huh?" I said aloud, hardly able to believe it.

Jen smiled her bright warm smile at me. How could this phone know Jen's face? Could it read my mind? Naturally I looked back.

Flames again. **GAME OVER.**

I didn't like this game anymore. It was too weird, too *impossible,* that Jen's face had appeared on the display. I resisted the impulse to call her and tell her. If she knew, it would only make her dislike the phone more. Anyway, it was too late to call.

I had better things to do with the time I had left than play games. I could try to see if the phone could do anything else—like maybe help me find a way to get the things the creepy guy wanted.

But why did I *want* to get the things he wanted? Why had that thought lodged itself in my mind? He was certainly dangerous. I should just ignore him. That's what absolutely everyone had told me to do.

The phone mewed. I looked at my watch. It was

after midnight. But that didn't mean anything to these crazy people. Should I answer it or not?

I couldn't resist.

"Hello?" I said, very tentatively.

I heard crying. "Trang? Help me, Trang! Fleck is coming. I know he is."

It just kept getting worse. The desperation in this woman's voice made me very scared for her. At the same time, after seeing Jen's face in that horrible game, I was beginning to feel more and more that turning the phone in was the only safe thing to do.

But maybe I could learn something useful from this woman to tell the police. "Calm down," I told her. "Who's Fleck?" I asked, though I was pretty certain he was the creepy guy. "What's he going to do?"

She just sobbed.

"Are you Lola?" I said.

I heard her gasp. The crying stopped. "Who are you?" she whispered. "Who told you my name?"

Now I was silent.

"Was it Fleck who told you my name?" She was getting hysterical again.

I wanted to make her trust me enough so that

she would explain what was going on. "He wanted me to get some stuff for the phone so he can get to where you are," I said.

"Oh, God!" she cried, her voice rising to a wail.

"What he wants me to get is impossible for me," I tried to reassure her. "Don't worry, I couldn't do it even if I wanted to. But if you want me to help you, then you have to tell me something."

"I have to go now," she said, her voice suddenly quiet. And she hung up.

After work on Saturday I rode my bike to Giga World, the biggest computer store anywhere around here.

I'd thought all night about what I should do. I didn't have enough information to take to the police. What could I tell them? A bunch of first names? Maybe they had the technology to trace the phone to Trang, or the authority to force the guy at the phone store to give them an address, but I knew better than to believe TV shows about cops who followed crazy hunches and tracked down the bad guys against all odds. The cops in my town might listen to me for five minutes, but they'd roll their eyes and toss the phone aside as soon as I left the station. I needed to find out more. When Fleck called next, I could tell him I'd gotten the stuff he wanted. It would be a way of getting him to talk. Somehow I knew he wouldn't believe a lie. I'd have to really have the stuff next to me to get him to answer my questions.

Was I crazy, or what? I had five dollars and some change. I wouldn't get my check from work until next Friday, and even then, it probably wouldn't be enough to buy the stuff Fleck wanted.

The parking lot was full, and there was only one space left on the bike rack—Saturday was the big day to go to Giga World. The place was going to be packed, and I hated going to crowded stores on the weekend. And yet, here I was.

You could hardly work your way down the aisles, it was so jammed. Of course, the management was too cheap to hire enough salespeople, and the harried ones there couldn't begin to handle all the impatient customers. Certainly none of them would pay any attention to a poorly dressed seventeen-year-old. Meaning there was nobody in this cavernous place I could ask where to find the stuff on my list. I would have to find it myself from the unhelpful signs over the dozens of aisles. And since I didn't have my own computer, and only used the ones at school, which were already preprogrammed and full of firewalls to block out anything interesting, I didn't know much about computer stuff and began to doubt that this was a good plan. I almost turned around and left as soon as I entered the store.

But for some reason I stayed in this incredibly irritating, crowded place, full of pushy people, and persevered. I just looked aisle by aisle, since the signs didn't mean much to me.

I kept glancing at my watch. Would Mom wonder where I was? She didn't work during the day on Saturday, but she had to leave at five. Usually on Saturdays I went over to Jen's after work, so Mom would probably assume that's where I was.

And then it hit me. I had forgotten to call Jen and tell her I wouldn't be coming over. That was very unusual—I never forgot to let her know, one way or the other, like from the pay phone at the hospital. Had I really forgotten? Or had I just pushed the thought of her out of my mind? That might be the weirdest part of all.

Squeezing past people, and being elbowed by the more aggressive ones, I minutely studied the contents of both sides of the aisles. I kept telling myself to just give up and get out of this horrible place. But some other part of me was too determined.

And finally, after about forty-five minutes, I came

across a section of flat cardboard containers, covered in plastic, with the word **FLASH**! written on them in red. Encased in the plastic was a small rectangular silver box, that had a green oblong window in the middle of it and coiled silver cords attached.

I read the information on the cardboard. It was a device for storing data. It held four gigabytes. It cost $80—impossibly out of my league.

But without the cardboard container, the whole thing would fit in my pocket.

Stop it! I almost said out loud. The last thing I needed was to get caught for shoplifting.

But cardboard and all would fit easily in my backpack. They had been too busy when I walked in to bother making me check the backpack, as they probably would normally have done. Would anybody notice me slipping it in? But even if nobody noticed, having an unsold item on me would probably set off an alarm on my way out.

I kept asking myself why I was doing this. Was I crazy, or what? Why did the mystery of the callers on the phone have this power over me?

And yet there I was, looking it over carefully, putting it back on its hanger, and then, without looking around, casually unzipping my backpack by feel and dropping the whole thing in. I strolled away, looking over other items hanging on the aisle. Nobody seemed to have noticed what I had done. And I couldn't help it—I felt that thrill of adventure in my gut that I had felt when I bought the phone. I had never done anything like this before.

But how big would the battery Fleck wanted be?

I found out after another half hour of squeezing my way through the avid, impatient people. The battery with the number Fleck wanted was also in a cardboard-and-plastic container. It was about an inch thick and three inches square. He had said I needed a certain kind of cable for the battery, and there they were, hanging next to the batteries, with some kind of small attachment on the ends of them that looked as if they might possibly fit into one of the orifices on the phone.

The battery was $99. The connecting cord was $5.99.

I didn't pay any attention. I wiped the sweat out of my eyes, got the phone out and checked. It looked like the connecting cord was the right size to fit into the bottom. The flash thing didn't seem like it would attach to the phone, but maybe there was a way of attaching it to the battery when it was in the phone.

If I ever got out of here with this stuff, that is. If I even *wanted* to get out of here with this stuff.

Again, I asked myself if I was crazy.

And again, I began to casually slip the battery into my backpack.

"Mommy! Mommy! Look at that man. He's putting stuff into his backpack. He's *stealing!*"

My heart thudded; sweat dripped into my eyes and stung. I fought the impulse to look and see whom the bratty little voice was coming from. Instead I moved slowly off in the opposite direction, which was unfortunately away from the entrance. I needed to put as many people as possible between me and this obnoxious kid. I didn't even know what he looked like, or if his mother was paying any attention to what he was telling her.

Then I felt a tap on my shoulder, and froze. My heart was pounding like crazy. But what else could I do except turn around?

"Excuse me," a woman said, studying me closely, looking stern.

I was about to defend myself, to ask her why she was bothering me, to tell her I was in a hurry. But I couldn't say a word.

And then she smiled, looking a little embarrassed, "I hope you don't mind, but you do look kind of like a computer geek, with that long hair and everything. Would you happen to know where they have the external floppy drives?"

And somehow, even though I wanted to run out of there in panic, I was able to play my part. I pointed. "In that aisle over there—aisle nine, I think—they have these flash things that are really small and hold as much as four gigabytes. Really cool. They cost $80, though. Too much for me."

"Thank you," she said. "I'll go and look." And she turned around.

Behind her I saw a little kid with glasses holding the hand of a frowning, stocky woman who was pointing angrily toward me, as she talked to a harried saleswoman. I turned and again forced myself to stroll, but more quickly this time, putting as many people as possible between me and the bratty kid and his mother, and the saleswoman they were pointing me out to. I turned the first corner, sliding past people, then turned another corner. Yeah, I hated crowds, but in this case the crowds were working to my advantage. When I dared to look back, I couldn't see the kid and his mother at all.

Now I just had to get out of this store. Was it alarmed or not? It was hard to imagine that it wouldn't be.

I made my way slowly through the crowds to the entrance, hoping that horrible kid and his mother wouldn't spot me again. My heart was thudding more than ever now. I approached the glass doors. Outside was sunlight and the normal world. If only I could make it out there!

And then I saw the guard, checking people's receipts. This was clearly impossible. I had to go back and somehow get the things out of my backpack and replace them, without anybody noticing. Why was I getting involved in all of this? I wasn't a hero, I was a kid trying to graduate from high school so I could go to college, get a good job, and afford to buy better things. Things like computers and the stuff I was about to try to steal.

Then I noticed that the guard at the other door was talking to one of the salesmen, both of them studying some papers. I walked past them. For some reason they didn't seem to notice me. And then I was outside.

An alarm went off, like a siren. I acted calm. I strolled over to the bike rack, the world blurred by sweat, unlocked my bike, hopped on, and started pedaling.

The guard and the salesman ran out of the store. "Hey, you!" the guard yelled at me. "Come back here. I didn't see your—"

And then I was behind a row of cars, pedaling faster. I was out of the parking lot in a flash and zooming up the street, wind blowing the sweat out of my eyes. I had done it! I had almost gotten caught, but I had done it!

Done what? I asked myself, continuing to pedal furiously, already out of breath. I had followed the orders of the creep on the other end of the phone—the creep who wanted to hurt that woman. That is, if she wasn't too hysterical and secretive to be believed. With that phone, it was hard to know what to believe.

I thought of seeing Jen's face in the hell game. I thought of how never before in my life had I ever stolen anything. What *was* this phone? And what was it doing to me?

It was after five when I got home, and Mom was gone. But there was a note by the phone. "Jen called," Mom had written in her scrawl. "Wondered where you were. Busy tonight with a family thing and can't see you."

I called Jen immediately from the regular phone—

Mom wasn't here, after all. Because of the cell phone, I had missed my chance to see Jen this afternoon. I didn't even think about how to explain, I just wanted her to know that I cared. But I got the answering machine, her mother's voice saying to leave a message. I just said I was sorry I hadn't called, there was a problem at work, and I hoped I could see her tomorrow.

I felt guiltier than ever as I hung up. I went into my room and got out the stuff I had stolen. It was spiffy and state-of-the-art, but it looked ugly to me now. I felt like I should go back to Giga World after it had closed and leave it just outside the door.

And what would I say if I turned on the phone and Fleck called? I should tell him I didn't get the stuff, of course. He'd be angry. But what could he do to me?

But somehow I knew I would tell him that I had it. I needed to know more.

I paced around the living room chair—there was nowhere else to move in the trailer—holding the cell phone, feeling lousy, not daring to turn it on, but also fighting the urge to do so. Things had gone from bad to worse. I thought of how intrigued I had been by the idea of **GAMES FROM REAL HELL**, and then how frightening the game had turned out to be, with Jen's face on it. Did that mean the phone was going to effect her and not just me? Was her mother right, that Jen wasn't safe, as long as I had it?

"Hell phone," I said out loud. That was the right name for it. That's what it was doing to my life. Hell phone.

But of course it wasn't long before I did turn it on. I went right to **GAMES FROM REAL HELL**, while I waited for Fleck to call.

This time I chose a different game: **TORTURE MASTER**. It was a list of names of instruments of torture that you had to match up with pictures. When you got one right, there was a colorful explosion, like a firework going off in the night sky, accompanied by a cry of pain. When you got one wrong, there was a droning buzz, and the phone actually gave you a little tingly electric shock. That was a pretty strong motivation for getting them right.

Luckily, most of them were easy, things I already knew. There was **STOCKS**, which you matched with a picture of a man standing in a wooden contraption that held his head and his arms locked in an uncomfortable position. The picture was very realistic; the man actually seemed to be alive and struggling to move and sweating. Another one I knew was **THE RACK**, which was a contraption that a person lay down upon and was tied to by his hands and feet. At either end were cranks that pulled on the person's arms and legs when they were turned by shadowy, hooded figures. When the person's arms and legs got dislocated from the sockets, you could hear her screaming, and also the cracking of her joints. It was extremely unpleasant.

But for some reason I kept going, on to **THE IRON MAIDEN OF NUREMBERG**. This was a box shaped like an upright coffin. The inside, and the double doors, were covered with long sharp metal spikes. As I watched, a man was led into the box, screaming and fighting. Dark shadowy figures pushed him inside. By some trick of photography, you could actually see what happened when the door was slowly shut, two spikes perfectly positioned to bore into his eyes, the rest of the spikes slowly penetrating the man's body from the back and the front, the blood oozing, then gushing out of a special drain at the bottom of the thing. The man died screaming in agony.

Why was I looking at this horrible stuff? What was the phone doing to me?

I kept getting shocked when I tried to match up

THE SCAVENGER'S DAUGHTER with the right picture, and getting it wrong. I got the colorful explosion and the scream of pain when I matched the words up with a large metal contraption like a giant twisted-up hairpin type thing. When the woman—who looked a lot like Jen's mother—was locked inside it, her head was strapped into an iron mask and forced between her knees, and her feet were held above her head. She was gasping and drooling, her tongue hanging out of the one opening in the mask, and you knew that when they took her out of that thing, she would never walk again.

This was too much. But now at least I knew some answers. This phone really had to be a hell phone. And I began to think that hell was where Fleck was calling me from.

Now I didn't even want to go to the police. I just wanted to get rid of this disgusting thing.

And then I remembered Lola's pleading voice. If I threw it away, I could never help her, and Fleck might really kill her. And if I didn't throw it away, there was a chance I could save her. What should I do?

I was about to turn the phone off in disgust when the display went blank and the phone rang.

If it was Lola, I would try to get her to tell me where she was. If it was Fleck, I didn't know what I would tell him. I pressed the green button. "Hello?"

"Did you get the stuff?"

"Why do you need it? What's this all about?"

"Forget it, kid. You're not putting anything over on me, with your wheedling ways. *When* you hook it up, and *if* I can see that it might work, then I'll tell you. Only then. Not a second before. Did you get the stuff?"

What should I say? Could I get him to tell me what was going on? "Er . . . yes. I got it."

"You said you didn't have any money. That must mean you stole it. Did you?"

"Yes!" And now I felt strangely angry. "I stole it. The first time in my life I ever did anything like that."

He chuckled. I couldn't remember if I'd ever heard him laugh before, but it wasn't a nice sound. "All the better. Good for you, chum. Stolen goods will work better for what I have in mind."

I didn't like the sound of that. And yet, at the same time, I felt flattered. "What do you have in mind?" I asked him.

"All in good time, all in good time," he said. "Are you ready to get to work now?"

I thought of Lola, how desperate she had sounded. "You're not going to kill anybody, or anything like that, are you?"

"Well, in fact, what I plan to do is exactly the *opposite* of that. You're going to help me. And that's all I'm going to say."

I was still confused, but his tone of voice made it clear he wasn't going to tell me anymore. "Why should I believe you?" I asked him.

"Because I'm an honest person. Like Jen."

"What?" My voice cracked with the shock of it. "What . . . How do you know about Jen?"

"I know all about your girlfriend, my good man. Pretty red hair, long legs, lovely smile, sweet . . . trusting . . . I wonder where she is right now. Do you know?"

"Leave her alone!" I yelled.

"Oh, I will. If you do what I want."

I hung up the phone and turned it off, my heart thudding. I had to think. Had this guy Fleck gotten to Jen? That wasn't possible, was it? He seemed to be trapped in hell, unable to get to Lola without my help, so there was no way he could get to Jen, right? He had to be bluffing, to get me to help him.

I picked up our phone and called Jen's house. The machine answered. "Jen," I said, trying not to sound too strange. "Call me when you get in, okay? I have to talk to you." I wished she had a cell phone, but her parents had refused to get her one. Now I had to wait.

At midnight, I was still waiting for the phone to ring. Jen should have been home by now. Her family didn't stay out late. I was sure Fleck was bluffing. But where was Jen?

I turned on the cell phone. I had to find out if Fleck had Jen. When the screen lit up, I saw the image of a girl with red hair locked in **THE SCAVENGER'S DAUGHTER.**

"No!" I screamed at the phone. The screen went dark and the phone mewed.

I answered it. "Ready to help?" Fleck asked.

"You don't have her! It isn't possible!" I yelled.

He didn't say anything.

"If you hurt her the slightest bit I'll . . . I'll—" I couldn't think of a threat that would work with him.

"Are you ready to help?" he said again.

"Yes." I was panting. "Don't hurt her."

"Fine. Good man. Now let's get to work. I can tell you exactly what to do—just like I told that little wipe Trang what to do, before he double-crossed me and stopped the process. The first thing to do is to have the battery and the connecting cord ready. You all set up?"

I was shaking. I hurried to my room and took them out of my backpack. It wasn't easy getting the stuff out of the sealed plastic. I had to go to the kitchen and get scissors, and the whole time Fleck was berating me about how long it was taking. "Come on, come on, hurry up!" he said irritably. "You don't know what I have to go through to get access to this contact. I can't talk all day. You should have been all prepared before you called me," he admonished me. "It's not like I've got forever, you know. I mean, I can tell you're a smart kid, pal. If you hurry up you will be amply rewarded . . . with a healthy girlfriend." He chuckled again.

With the scissors, I had finally gotten the battery

and the power cord packages open. There was an inevitability to doing this that began to calm me.

"Okay, now you plug the flat metal end of the power cable into the narrow oblong slot in the battery, you see that? Plug it in so that the little design is facing upward, toward the metal top of the battery, not the black bottom. Got that?"

I didn't know much about computers, but this part was easy. "Done," I said, and through my fear for Jen I couldn't help feeling proud.

"Brilliant," he said. "Now you can see that the other end of the power cable is small and round. It goes right into the hole in the bottom of the phone. Now you just slide it in there, nice and easy." The way he said it sounded vaguely obscene, but it went in easily enough.

"Now you have the flash all ready, don't you, pal?"

I didn't. It was still encased in plastic. "I have to open it with scissors," I said, feeling frantic, the phone cradled against my shoulder as I hurried for the scissors again.

"You should have had it all set up before you called me," he said again. "I thought you were smart."

"You called me," I couldn't help pointing out.

"Just hurry up!"

I struggled to get the flash thing and its cable out without cutting the cable with the scissors. "There," I said. "Got it."

"Okay. Now all you have to do with your brilliant little mind is plug the flash into the flat end of the cable, and plug the pointy end of the cable into the round hole on the side of the battery. See that?"

"Hold on. I have to think. I only have two hands."

"Only two hands? You poor thing. You should see how many hands some of the folks around here have."

It made me shiver that he could joke with me like this while threatening to hurt Jen. I followed his directions and connected the flash to the battery. It had seemed like it would be hard at first, but now, somehow, it was easy to hold all this equipment even in one hand, as if it had been designed to fit together.

Now that I had finished the last step, I had the sensation that I was making a horrible mistake, that this was all a trick. The display on the phone, usually a pale gray, turned bright red. I put the phone to my ear.

Fleck was laughing. "You did it! You did it, man! I can feel it from here. I can see you from here. Not a bad looking kid, except for all that hair. Maybe this is really going to work!"

My heart sank. "*What's* going to work? Where's Jen?"

"I'm getting the hell out of here," he said, "if you'll pardon the expression. Whatever you do, don't hang up. And don't look behind you, if you want to see your girlfriend again. Stand facing the front door. Go and stand facing the front door. Don't look behind."

That reminded me of something, but at the moment I was too distracted to remember what it was. Now, under his voice, the phone was making all kinds of funny bleeping and crackling noises. They got louder and louder—so loud I had to hold the phone away from my ear. I was amazed again by how easy it was to hold all this equipment in one hand.

Suddenly the phone screeched so loud I was afraid it would break my eardrum.

"Press the big key in the middle. Start at the top and press each side in a clockwise direction. Keep doing it, as fast as possible."

I could barely hear him above the screeching phone, just enough to be able to do what he said. Each time I pressed a different side of the key, the color on the display changed, red to blue to purple to green. The second time around it became striped with many colors. The third time around the stripes began to move, up and down, up and down. Then they began to spin in a dizzying way. I felt like I was falling into it, like it was sucking me in, and squeezed my eyes shut.

"No, no, don't watch the display, watch the door!" Fleck bellowed at me. "And don't look back!"

Something in the trailer creaked behind me and I almost looked back. Then I remembered the game of escaping from hell, walking up the tunnel without looking back, and managed to control the impulse to turn and look behind. I blinked and watched the door. The phone screeched even louder and then went dead.

There was a knock on the door.

7

The sudden silence was a shock, though my ear was still ringing.

The knock on the door came again, impatient.

I stood there paralyzed, still holding the phone. Was it Fleck at the door?

It had to be. Impossible as it seemed that a phone could move someone through space, even with this extra equipment, it had to be Fleck. The phone had just done all these other crazy things, after all.

And now that Fleck was only a few feet away from me, I was more scared than ever. Once I let him in, what would he do to me? Even if he didn't hurt me, would I be able to get rid of him before Mom came home? He was so pushy, and somehow he always got his way—I had done everything he had asked me to.

Only Trang had gotten away from him. And if I could believe Fleck, Trang was now toast.

Worst of all were the threats he had made about Jen. If he got the phone away from me, would he be able to carry them out? *Had* he carried them out?

I had gotten myself in really deep. And it was all my own fault. If only, if *only* I had never bought this phone.

But if I hadn't, Lola might die. All I could tell from her incoherent wailing was that Trang seemed to have deserted her.

The next knock was a bang. The whole flimsy trailer shook.

I moved slowly toward the door in a kind of trance. I unlocked it. Trying not to think, I pulled it open.

A naked man stood there. He stank, he reeked, it was all I could do not to retch and squeeze my nose shut with my fingers. He was shaven bald, but I could tell from the stubble on his head that his hair was black. His wiry yet emaciated body was covered in bruises and awful-looking blistered burns and sores and rashes. And cuts, deep jagged cuts, and places where the skin hung off his flesh, some of them seeping blood. There was a heavy film of grease, soot, and dust all over him. He had a sharp nose and a narrow chin and piercing green eyes. One of his eyes was black and red and swollen and half shut.

He spread his arms and looked down at himself. "And to think, the ladies used to say I was good-looking," he said. It was Fleck's voice all right.

I just stood there. "What . . . what happened to you?" I said.

"This is the way we live, where I come from—where you got me out of. Well? Are you just going to stand there? Aren't you going to be hospitable and invite me in?"

"I better hose you off first. The place would be filthy as soon as you took a step inside."

He shrugged as if he couldn't care less, and stepped back out into the yard, limping slightly. I don't know what I had expected but it sure hadn't been this. "Wait there a minute," I said. I put the phone down on the table where I always ate. Then I went outside and turned on the hose faucet and sprayed him with water. "Aaah!" He lifted his chin and closed his eyes, as water dripped down his face. "Man that feels good! Clean water! A real shower! Water without crap in it! After all these years."

"You'll have to take another one inside," I said,

when I could get him as clean as I could without soap. "Wait here for a second." I went in and got a dirty towel so he could wipe off his feet so they wouldn't mark up the linoleum floor. He obliged. Then I led him into the bathroom. I left him alone while he showered, then cleaned out the tub as best as I could while he stood and watched. It would need another cleaning before Mom came home. But at least he didn't smell quite so bad anymore.

A stupid thought flashed through my mind: Where was he going to sit? Anything he sat on would get bloody.

"Well? Aren't you going to offer me anything? They're very stingy with food and water where I come from. Only enough to keep you from passing out and missing all the fun."

The chairs at the kitchen table were faded red plastic. I quickly got a couple of rags and put them down on one of the chairs. "Here. Sit down. Mom would be pissed if you got blood on anything. She'd want to know where it came from. I'd have to tell her about you and—"

He grabbed me by the neck of my T-shirt. "You're not going to tell anybody anything. And get me something to wear—a pair of shorts, anything." He snickered. "I mean, not that this cool, clean air and water doesn't feel refreshing and all. But I'm embarrassed to be naked in front of somebody who's dressed. I'm taller than you but thinner. Anything you can wear will fit me well enough to cover up some of this loveliness."

I gulped. The sight of him *was* pretty sickening, even though he didn't stink so much anymore. Maybe I could find something for him to wear, and something for him to eat and drink. But with him around I didn't feel like eating anything myself.

I got him a pair of running shorts and my oldest, most threadbare T-shirt. When I came back with them he was just putting down the phone. I didn't want him touching it. Who knew what he could do with it, with all that equipment on it now? I had to check on Jen.

I threw the clothes at him and took the phone without a word and went into my room and closed the door. It was one A.M. now, an impossible time to call Jen, but I had to know if she was safe—nothing was more important than that. I called her number.

After several rings her father's sleepy voice came on. "Wha . . . ? Who is this?" he said.

"Mr. Golding. Sorry. It's . . . it's Nick. It's just that

. . . Jen didn't return my call. Can I talk to her? She's home, isn't she?"

"Of course she's home. It's way past her curfew—and way past a decent time for *anyone* to call this house. That phone is not making you very popular around here, young man. Not popular at all!" And he hung up. He had never spoken to me like that before.

I was relieved that Jen was safe, but angry that I'd had to antagonize her father to find out. Cursing under my breath, I put the phone in my backpack, and then put the backpack in the closet, and piled stuff on top of it. I didn't want Fleck to get his hands on it. He had tricked me by showing me that picture of Jen being tortured, but now I knew she was really safe. And she was going to stay that way.

When I came back he was wearing the clothes, and chuckling. "So you called my bluff. Now you know your gorgeous girlfriend is all safe and sound. But she might not always be."

Of course he had overheard the conversation with Jen's father. I bit my lip, not trusting myself to speak, I was so furious. Now Jen's father was mad at me and it was all Fleck's fault. And she would always be in danger, as long as he was around. I gestured roughly at the chair with the rags on it and he sat down gingerly, as if his bruises were painful. "I told you, I need something to eat," he said.

"I don't care what you need!" I said. "Why did you show me that picture of Jen in that horrible machine? Why did you threaten her?"

Suddenly he was very serious. "Would you have brought me back here if I hadn't?" he asked me.

Angry as I was, I thought about that. "Well . . . probably not," I said honestly.

He lifted his hands. "I had to get back here to help Lola. She's in danger for her life, and Trang seems to have deserted her. You were the one with the phone. What choice did I have?"

"But Lola's afraid of *you!*" I burst out.

"Is she? Did she ever say that? Think about it."

I tried as best I could to remember the two times she had called. And in fact she had never said anything directly about being afraid of Fleck. Only that she needed help, and Trang was gone.

"You came back here to *help* Lola?" I said. "But what's she in danger from? And how did you find out about Jen? And—"

"I can't help anybody, or keep answering your endless questions, until I get something to eat. Look at me! Can't you see I'm on the verge of starving to death? They keep us that way on purpose."

I sighed. But I couldn't argue with him. "Well, you want some dried noodles? That's about all we have."

"Anything you got. And water," he said. "Right away. A big, big glass of water. Nice and *cold*."

I put some ice cubes in a glass and filled it from the tap. He swallowed it down in one huge gulp and banged the glass on the table for more, and I gave him more. He drank the second glass a little more slowly. I got the noodles out of the cupboard. It gave me something to do while I wondered how much I could trust him. Not much, I was sure.

"Well? Don't you want to know?" he asked me. "I told you I'd tell you where I was if you got me out of there." He made a questioning gesture with his swollen, blistered fingers. I noticed he was missing some fingernails. Had they taken them off slowly?

"Well, you *look* like you were in a concentration camp or something, or a CIA prison where they torture people, but I don't think that's the answer."

"You don't think that's the answer?" he mocked. "I suppose you could call it a sort of concentration camp. The worst concentration camp the world has ever known. All the human ones, throughout history and into the future, are fun fairs compared to this place. Can you hurry up with those noodles? I told you they don't feed us much."

"The heat's on high. I can't make it go any faster. Were you . . . were you in *hell?*" I dared to say.

"You got it, buddy. And believe you me, what I did in this world, that I thought I wanted so much, sure as hell wasn't worth going there for."

"But I just did something wrong today," I said, suddenly more scared than ever. "I stole that stuff. If I'd known hell was real, I never would have done something like that."

He waved a hand at me. "Child's play. You don't spend an eternity in hell for stealing a few pieces of electronic equipment. Anyway, you were doing it to help somebody. That cancels it out. Remember that." He gave me a hard stare. "This is the most important thing I can ever tell you. Are you listening?"

I nodded.

"Whatever you do," he said slowly, "if your motivation is to *help* somebody, then you don't go to hell. Will you remember that?"

I nodded again.

He kept staring at me hard. "Do not forget it, no

matter what. If your motivation is to help, then you don't go to hell."

The water was boiling now. It gave me a chance to look away from his uncomfortable stare. Was he telling me the truth, that you didn't go to hell if your motivation was to help somebody? I dumped the package of noodles into a bowl and poured the water over them and got a spoon and fork and put it all down in front of him. I looked at my watch. It was one-thirty. I would have to work fast to get him hidden somehow. Mom would be back by two-thirty at the latest.

He gulped down the noodles like he was starving, hot as they were. The bowl was empty in less than a minute. "Got anymore?" he said.

If I gave him another one there wouldn't be enough for me. Mom kept her eyes on stuff like how many bags of noodles we had, and I never ate more than two. But it didn't matter because I knew I couldn't eat with him anywhere near me, or even the thought of him on my mind.

How was I going to get rid of him before Mom came home? Where could he possibly go, looking like this and without any money?

But before I got to that hard question, there were

other things I wanted to find out. "How . . . how did you know how to get out? I thought there was no escape."

"If you keep being obedient, you'll find out."

I sighed. I felt so frustrated that I said, "I just did you this huge favor, and you still won't answer a simple question?"

"You haven't done the main favor yet."

Was the main favor going to be what he had said about saving Lola? Was it the truth or a lie? "Main favor?" I asked, feeling a chill. "What's this main favor going to be?"

"You sure ask a lot of questions. Where's those other noodles?"

It was clear that I wasn't going to get any answers out of him. I sighed again and gave him his second bowl of soup, which he gulped down. He slugged down another glass of water. Then he leaned carefully back in the chair. "Oh, that's better, that's way, way better. You're a little angel of mercy, even with all that dumb-looking kinky blond hair."

I was insulted. But that's what he wanted me to feel. "What's this main favor going to be?" I asked him again.

He waved the question away with his hand. "You

may be up to it, you did such a good job with the phone. You must be really smart."

Now he was distracting me, but I fell for it—I couldn't help feeling flattered. "Well, I do get good grades, even though I can't afford to have my own computer, and have to work after school. If I didn't, I couldn't get a scholarship to college and I'd have to live in a place like this all my life."

He glanced around the trailer as if he hadn't even noticed it before. I didn't blame him for being preoccupied with food and clothing. "It's a palace compared to where I've been. I'll do very well here, thank you."

I was about to tell him he couldn't stay here, the trailer was too small. Then I realized I didn't trust him to stay anywhere else—at least not for now. He had found out about Jen. And I wasn't sure he really wanted to save Lola. I had brought him here and now he was my responsibility. I had to keep an eye on him.

"Well . . . for tonight, maybe you could scrunch up under my bed," I said. "After that, we'll have to come up with something else or my mother will figure it out."

He drummed his fingers on the plastic table top.

“So we have a little problem after tonight,” he said. “Okay, so I lucked out because somebody smart ended up with the doctored phone. But I *unlucked* out because he’s just a kid who doesn’t have a place to stay. Lola’s no good, of course. She’d never trust me. Maybe Trang. Trang has to be the answer.”

“You said Trang was toast.”

“I just said that to scare the new owner of the phone. I was smart enough to make calls from down there to a doctored phone up here, I was smart enough to have it doctored even more, more things deleted, so there’d be room on it to get me out—though I’m not the first person to ever get out—but what I *couldn’t* do from down there is turn anybody up here into toast.” He paused, and gave me a hard look with his green, green eyes. “Not until I physically got here. Where I now am.”

I shivered, thinking of Jen. I already knew this guy would do anything to get what he wanted.

“Yeah, so it’s got to be that poor little wipe Trang, who was so afraid to help me that he chickened out. If we can ever find him. I couldn’t know where Trang went once he returned the phone—I could only communicate with the person who had the phone. But he must have left a trail. They always do." He rested his chin gingerly on his hand and thought.

"Well, we better get you hidden now. My mother will be home soon. And you don't want her to find you anymore than I do." It was impossible to imagine *what* she would do if she saw him here.

We got him squeezed under my bed. It was tight, but he seemed used to tight places. I quickly cleaned out the bathroom a second time, threw out the rags, then went back to my dark bedroom. I turned on the little radio so that we could talk quietly, while I listened for the sound of Mom coming back.

"Where's the phone?" he asked me.

I was afraid of this. I didn't trust him with it. "Er . . . there's a secret place where I keep it," I said. Now I was being the evasive one.

He shrugged. "I don't need it that much, now that I'm here. But you might see if you can find any clues about Trang on it."

I was curious about what this main favor was that he had in mind for me. But I had already learned that I couldn't ask him directly. And there was also something else on my mind. "Why did the caller ID have to be disabled?" I asked him. "It sure is inconvenient not knowing who's calling on it."

"Because obsolete instruments like that can only do a certain number of things. The caller ID was one thing I didn't think it needed. Along with a lot of others. When Trang got rid of them, that made more space for other data that could help get me back here. Did Trang ever call you?"

I didn't see why I shouldn't tell him. "Yeah."

"Then he might call again, give us some clues." Then he chuckled his scary yet infectious chuckle. "There's a certain irony to the fact that your name is Nick, I have to say. Nick is a mythical name for the big boss down there. So I escaped from one and ended up with another."

How did he even know my name? How did he know about Jen? But another question was uppermost in my mind.

"Are the bosses in hell just going to let you get away and stay here? Aren't they going to try to get you back?"

"Yeah, they're going to try. But it always takes them awhile—they're not too bright. If they give me enough time to do what I have to do, with the main favor from you, then I hope I'll never have to go back there again."

Then I couldn't keep from asking, "Okay, I can see you're pretty badly beaten up. Obviously they torture you down there. But what's it like? I mean what does it *look* like? Like flames? Like pools of shit up to your chin and people saying, 'Don't make waves?' And like devils with pitchforks?"

Suddenly his tone became serious in the darkness. It made me very uncomfortable that he was lying hidden right beneath me. "Don't make old jokes about it. It's about the most *unfunny* place you could ever imagine. And it's not easy to describe. Nothing like earth. Nothing green, nothing growing, nothing alive. You could say it's sort of like a battlefield that's been wiped out with Agent Orange and napalm, except in battles people were lucky and died. There you can't die, it just goes on hurting, more than you think you can bear. But people were right about one thing—good old Dante. There are different degrees. And don't ask me which one I was in."

"What did you do—"

"Jeez, you're just full of questions, aren't you? I think I've told you enough for the time being. I'm getting tired. All the beatings and torture were one thing. But getting out through that phone takes a lot out of you."

"Fine. We better stop talking anyway. Mom will be home any minute."

“You’ll give me something to eat in the morning?” he asked me sleepily, almost sounding pathetic.

“Tomorrow I can do that,” I told him. “It’s Sunday and Mom has a busy day at work—big restaurant day, from breakfast all the way through. But on Monday I have to go to school. We’re going to have to find you someplace else by then.”

He was already snoring softly.

From the backpack in the closet the phone mewed. Fleck continued to snore. I would have to whisper in order not to wake him up.

I scrambled to find and unzip the backpack. Maybe it would be Trang. Maybe I could foist Fleck off on him—I wanted to get rid of him more than anything, and Trang was the only person I could think of who could keep an eye on him for me, and prevent him from hurting Jen or Lola. I pressed the green button. “Hello?” I whispered.

The sound of sobbing. “What’s happening? Did he call you again?”

My heart sank. Lola. Had I put her in danger by bringing Fleck back? Did I dare to tell her what had really happened?

“What are you hiding?” Her voice began to rise to its usual hysteria. “Did Fleck call you?”

"He . . . asked me to get some stuff to fix up the phone."

"Did you?"

"I don't have any money." I felt terrible lying to her, she was so frightened. But what if I'd done the wrong thing? She wouldn't trust me to help her if Fleck was planning on killing her and I told her I'd brought him back. I had to lie.

"I feel like a sitting duck here. I've told the police, but they don't believe me, they won't give me a twenty-four-hour guard. I'm completely helpless." She started to cry again.

Was she being held prisoner? How did she think I could help her? And what was Fleck going to try to make me do? Help her or hurt her?

"Are you being held prisoner? Why can't you run away and hide? Does the person you're afraid of know where you live?"

"He . . . he knows everything," she could barely say, sobbing now. She hung up before I could ask her where she was.

I heard the trailer door open. Mom. "Nick? Did I hear you talking to somebody?" I could hear at once that Mom was in a really bad mood

"I must have been talking in my sleep," I called

out, trying to sound drowsy. I wanted her to think I was asleep and leave me alone.

"Nick! Come into the bathroom. Now!"

I rumpled my hair so it would look like I'd been asleep and went into the bathroom.

She was standing by the shower, wrinkling her nose. "What's that smell—that awful garbagey toilet smell? What have you been doing here anyway?"

Now what was I going to say?

I had to think fast. "Er . . . I ate too many noodles, too fast. They must have been old. I got sick and threw up a lot."

"I always check the dates when I buy them," she said. "And you haven't been sick like that in years."

I sighed. "Look at me," I said. "Do I *look* healthy?"

The sight of Fleck had been sickening, all right, and her face changed as she looked more closely at me. "You do look like you had a kind of a shock," she said, and sighed. "Just what I need."

"I'll be fine tomorrow—I feel a lot better already," I said, hoping I had distracted her from the smell in the bathroom. "I just need some sleep."

But exhausted as I was, I had trouble dozing off. First of all, I hated having Fleck right underneath me.

But mainly I worried about keeping an eye on him, and preventing him from hurting anybody. If by some miracle we were able to find Trang, could I trust him to do that for me? He had told me not to listen to Fleck. But had he really meant it? Could he be Fleck's friend and possible accomplice?

I hardly slept at all.

In the early morning I thought of it: The only things on the phone besides the hell games were the Vietnamese songs. If there was any clue on the phone about Trang, it had to be there. I got up and dug the phone out of my backpack. I looked at the songs again. They were impossible for me to read, of course. I went back to bed

Despite having worked so late, Mom had to get up early for the Sunday breakfast shift. At least I didn't work on Sundays. I stayed in bed until she was gone. I didn't know whether Fleck was awake or asleep but he wasn't making a sound.

I got up quietly and took the phone outside to call Jen. I was nervous about it, after waking her father up last night, but the longer I waited to apologize the harder it would get. I also wanted to warn her to be careful. I had to let her know why I hadn't seen her yesterday and that I was busy today. I would have to be vague about it all, to lie as little as possible. I hated the idea of lying to her. But how could I tell her about Fleck?

As usual, her mother answered. As soon as she heard my voice she said, "Haven't you bothered us enough, after waking us up in the middle of the night? And are you calling on that awful phone?"

"I'm sorry about last night. I called to apologize; I was just concerned because I hadn't heard from Jen. I haven't turned that phone on since I was at your house." It wasn't easy lying to her mother, but it wasn't like lying to Jen. "And I'm taking it to the sanitation department tomorrow. For sure. I don't want to have anything to do with it anymore." That wasn't a lie. I really wanted to get rid of it—except my conscience told me I had to keep it in order to help Lola. Even though I didn't know her, I still felt it was my responsibility, as the one with the phone and the one who had helped Fleck, to protect her. She was so pathetic and frightened.

"Are you sure you're getting rid of it?" Jen's mother said suspiciously.

I wanted to yell at her but of course I couldn't. "Look, I learned. That phone has to go. I'll drop it off as soon as school is over. That's a promise."

"Well . . ." she said.

"Please," I said. "I have to go to work soon—I need the extra money now. I just want to talk to Jen for a second."

"Oh, I'm sorry. She's not here."

She had to be at practice. Where else could she be? "Did the coach call or something?" I asked.

"No. A young man called her last night. She met him when the soccer team was playing at another school. He came and picked her up today in his new car. A fine young man."

I hated the way she said "a fine young man" so smugly. And why would Jen go out with somebody else, without telling me—somebody with his own car? I was too stunned for a moment to think of anything to say. And worried. I didn't like Jen going off with strangers, now that Fleck was around. Finally I asked, "Do you know when she'll be back? I'd like to talk to her for a minute."

"Sometime this afternoon. Not late," her mother said, as if it were nothing that Jen had gone out with somebody else.

"Okay, thanks," I muttered, and hung up.

What was going on? I couldn't imagine Jen doing this without telling me first, at least.

Back in the trailer, I could hear Fleck in the bathroom. I hid the phone and got out some dry cereal for him—I knew he would demand food immediately.

He came out of the bathroom, stretching luxuriantly. "Best night of sleep I've had in forever," he said. "Down where I came from they play drunk people singing karaoke on blaring loudspeakers all night. Enough to drive you out of your mind. Man, it was heaven lying in this quiet trailer and—"

"Why did Jen go out with somebody else without telling me? Did you have anything to do with it?"

He grinned at me with an evil twinkle in his eye. His face looked a little less awful now, after a good night's sleep, and with some of the sores beginning to heal. "She's not on my agenda, pal. I told you I had to pretend that I could hurt her so you'd help me get out of hell. I certainly wouldn't do her any harm now that you're on my team." He clamped his hand on my shoulder like we were best buddies, and I knew he wasn't going to say another word on the subject.

I had to figure out what he was up to. Trang was my only hope. "Listen," I said. "I was thinking about the phone. And there *is* something on it that looks like a list of songs in some other language,

Vietnamese I think. You think there might be a clue about Trang there?" I sighed. "Too bad it's in Vietnamese."

"I can read Vietnamese. I made a point of learning it. I also made a point of not telling Trang I knew it. It's always the best policy to tell as little about yourself as possible."

He sure was good at that. I still had no idea what he had done to get to hell, how he knew how to get out, and what his real plans were—especially what he had in mind for me.

"Is that a box of Cheerios I see in your hot little hand? Could they be for me? I need the strength. If we want to find Trang today."

Finally he was making sense. "Yeah. I'm being kind and giving you my portion. My mother notices how fast food gets eaten up—she has to, because she doesn't have any money. Not that I could eat anywhere near you anyway, no offense. Even after I cleaned up last night, my mother noticed the smell. I had to tell her I threw up.

"Then hand them over," he said, not even thanking me. I dumped the cereal into a bowl, then looked away as he wolfed it down.

"Ah, that's better," he said.

Even though his bruises were healing slightly he needed a shave more than ever now, and looked really grubby. If we were going to find Trang, we might have to be around other people, too. What would they think? I was embarrassed to admit to myself that I really didn't want to be seen with him.

"I don't suppose you have a car or anything?" he asked me.

"My mother has an old wreck that she uses all the time. All I have is my bike," I told him, thinking about the guy with the car who Jen was with right this minute.

"Then get the phone out of its hiding place and let me see that list you were talking about. Just for a sec. If you really want to get me another place to stay."

I didn't want to give him the phone—I hated the thought of him touching it. But what choice did I have? I couldn't read Vietnamese, and he could. I went to my bedroom and got it out. In the living room I turned it on. It mewed.

I pressed the green button. "Hello?"

"Oh. You do not throw away yet?" said the heavily accented male voice.

"No. I still have it," I said slowly, so he would understand. "I'm very glad you called. Please don't hang up." This was the best thing that could have happened. And I wasn't going to ask Fleck what I should say. I knew what I wanted and I didn't care if he wanted something different. "Please. Do you have a car? I have to talk to you directly, face to face, but I don't have a car."

"Well . . . yeah, I have car," he said reluctantly.

I glanced over at Fleck, who was watching me intensely, then looked away from him. I didn't care what he wanted. What I wanted was to protect Jen and help Lola. "Please come and get me," I said to the man with the heavy accent, who had to be Trang. "Please. Remember, it's your fault I have this phone. It's your fault they're calling me. You owe it to me to help me just a little. To explain. Just come here and talk for a couple of minutes. I want to help Lola."

"She poor lady, very afraid. But don't know if you can trust her."

That surprised me—I had assumed Lola was a victim until now. "Then you need to explain it to me."

"Well . . ."

"Please. You *have* to!" I said. "This is where I live." I gave him the directions to the trailer, very slowly, and when I was finished I repeated them again, to make sure he understood. I kept not looking at Fleck.

I didn't tell Trang about Fleck because I didn't know if he was his enemy or his friend, and I didn't want to frighten him off. I just knew I had to have help to deal with Fleck, and I was willing to take the chance that Trang might be on my side.

Trang sighed. "Okay, okay. I come like you ask me. But only one time. And only for short time. Take me half hour."

"Thank you, thank you. I just want to talk. I'll be ready. You're are really coming now?"

Another sigh. "Yes, I come now." We hung up. I turned and looked back at Fleck to see what his reaction was.

His face was lit up with a smile so bright he almost didn't look hideous. "Brilliant! Absolutely perfect!" he congratulated me.

Now I wondered if I *had* done the right thing. Could anything Fleck liked be the right thing? What did Trang mean about not trusting Lola, who always seemed so afraid? And what was going to happen to this poor Trang guy now?

I told myself that wasn't my problem. He had known them before I had. They were more his responsibility than mine. And after I got Fleck out of here, I could figure out how to deal with the situation with Jen and this other guy—and help Lola, too, if that seemed possible. It was my only reason for keeping the phone.

I waited in front of the house and Fleck hid behind the one bush next to the trailer, so the neighbors wouldn't see him.

A half an hour went by and Trang didn't show up. Five more minutes went by, and then ten. I began to worry that he had gotten lost, or had just lied to me and wasn't coming at all. What was to stop him from doing that? Then I'd really be sunk. I couldn't call him. Another five minutes went by and I felt a growing knot at the pit of my stomach.

I darted behind the bush for a second, still keeping my eyes on the road. "Is he bad at directions?" I asked Fleck. "Do you think he got lost? Does he always do what he says he will?"

"He's an obedient little twerp, but he's dim. He'll probably have trouble finding the place, but he'll get here if he said he would."

"He'd better," I muttered.

And a few minutes later a dented, rusty old car with a cracked windshield came slowly around the corner. I could just see an Asian face inside, wearing glasses and peering ahead over the steering wheel.

"That's him," Fleck hissed from behind the bush.

I ran toward the car, waving my arms. "Here I am! This is the place!" I shouted.

The car stopped. The man rolled down the window. I peered in at him. He was middle-aged, and wearing synthetic brown pants and a brightly patterned red synthetic shirt that didn't match and an old threadbare jacket, and had on thick, black-framed glasses. "You are one with phone?" he asked me.

"Yes, that's me," I said eagerly. "My name's Nick. You are Trang?"

He nodded sadly.

"You came to the right place," I said. "Thank you so much. I just needed to talk to you for a few—"

The back door of the car opened, and Fleck zipped in and slammed it behind himself. "Get in, Nick. Here we go," he said.

Trang recoiled in horror at what was in his back seat, then turned to me with a baffled and miserable expression as I got into the car. "What is . . . that? Why you lie to me?"

"You don't recognize him? But I thought . . ."

Trang looked again. Then his mouth dropped

open. "So . . . so different now. But, yes, it is him." He turned back to me. "You helped him!" He sounded positively angry at me.

"Forget about that. Take us to Lola's," Fleck ordered him.

9

The car lurched abruptly into our driveway, then backed sloppily out, running over what was meant to be a lawn, and turned around. As he was doing this, Trang lit a cigarette, which made his driving even worse. He headed back out of the trailer park, driving too fast for this narrow gravel road.

He had been angry at me for getting Fleck out of hell—and yet it seemed that he was immediately obeying Fleck's order. Whose side was he on, anyway? He had told me he didn't know if I could trust Lola, either. Was there *anybody* I could trust? Or were they all lying to me about everything?

And meanwhile, Jen was out with this "fine young man" who had a new car. What was I going to do about that?

I turned to Fleck in the back. "What are we doing? I'm not going to help you hurt anyone."

"I told you, I'm not the one Lola's in danger from. She doesn't like me much, but she knows I can help her. I'm not the threat to her life."

"Then who is?"

"Enough questions!" He clamped his mouth shut in that way that indicated I wasn't going to get another answer out of him.

The car grunted to a stop at the intersection where the small road from the trailer park met the busy paved four-lane road. It was a dangerous intersection, and Trang was an unusually bad driver. And now it seemed he had to make a left turn, and there was no stop sign or light on the main road. It was Sunday, but there was still a lot of traffic.

Trang suddenly jolted out into the middle of the traffic. Horns honked madly. Tires squealed as cars tried to stop. I squeezed my eyes shut. Somehow we made it without another car hitting us.

"I see your driving hasn't gotten any better," Fleck said dryly. "Try not to kill me, okay? I just got back here."

Trang continued driving too fast, veering between lanes, smoking. The car reeked sickeningly of cigarette smoke. He jerked his head at me. "You think Lola trust him? She don't trust nobody but me and cops—and cops don't listen to her."

"She's been calling you, hasn't she, Nick?" Fleck said.

"Yes. She keeps crying and she sounds really afraid of something. I thought it was you, but you say you're going to help her."

"Don't try to trick me into telling you too much," was all he would say.

"Well, I'll find out from *her* then," I said, feeling angry about everything now. What if she was going to be as evasive as Fleck? I kept telling myself I was keeping the phone to help Lola, but then why had I brought Fleck here? Because he had threatened to hurt Jen. I could see that he was dangerous in that way, and that I had made a disastrous mistake. It was all so confusing.

And because of all of them I was spending time away from Jen, possibly putting her in danger. If it seemed like Lola was just playing games with me, too, I would leave and find Jen.

We passed a car on the left with only an inch to spare. The car honked furiously. Trang tossed his cigarette out the window and lit another one, the car wobbling as he did. "How far away does she live?" I asked. I couldn't take this for very long.

"Getting a little nervous, Nick?" Fleck asked me, and chuckled. Trang seemed totally impervious to the effect his driving was having on us.

"I just want to know how far away she lives," I snapped at him. "How can you hide that from me if we're going there?"

They both continued to ignore my question. "You still have that pathetic part-time job doing errands for Lola?" Fleck asked Trang.

"Yes, but I live in different place now. Hiding from you."

"Well that's *great*, Trang ol' boy!" Fleck said gaily. "Now I have a place to stay. And I can borrow your clothes and shave with your razor and brush my teeth with your toothbrush and use your car." He slapped Trang on the shoulder. Trang winced. And who wouldn't? Being touched by Fleck was bad enough, but the thought of sharing clothes and a razor with him—not to mention a toothbrush!—was a nightmare.

Trang had squealed around several corners by this time, and we were now in a residential neighborhood. That gave me hope. The neighborhood was better than the trailer park, but nothing like Jen's. It was mostly big, anonymous brick apartment buildings. Like all the people who called me on this phone—I was beginning to think of them as "the Callers"—Lola didn't seem to have much money.

"Park here," Fleck said suddenly. A tree and a high row of hedges blocked the car from the view of any of the buildings. Did he not want Lola to see us coming?

Trang stopped with a screech of tires and then very awkwardly, a smoking cigarette dangling from his mouth, parallel parked in a large space that would have been easy for anyone else to get into, but was a struggle for him.

"I'm not going in, of course," Fleck said. "Even though I'm going to help her, she won't believe that. She'll be afraid of me and won't let anyone in. You two go. And don't take forever. Just let her meet Nick and explain whatever she wants to tell him—if anything. I'll be dying of boredom waiting for you. And then we have to get Nick home before we can go to your place, Trang, wherever it is, and I can clean up some more. It's not a whole lot of fun being totally repellent."

Trang and I walked about half a block in silence. He seemed nervous, chewing on his fingernails. He had to be on Lola's side, if he was working for her. But then why was he apparently going to go along with what Fleck wanted? And why was Lola afraid of Fleck, if someone else was the real threat to her?

Lola's building was a cheap, brick apartment house like all the others. From the bell Trang pushed I could see that her apartment was on the top, the fourth floor. After a pause, the female voice I recognized from the phone said, "Yes? Who is it?" As usual, she sounded scared.

"Trang. And boy with phone, name Nick."

Another pause. "Are . . . are you sure? How can you be sure it's him? What happened?"

"I know is boy with phone because I call number and he tell me where to come and get him. He want meet you—and you want meet him, too, I think."

"You're sure?" she asked again. Okay, she was afraid, she was in distress, and it was my duty to help her, and I couldn't shirk it. But like all of the Callers, she got on my nerves.

"Can you show me?" he asked me, not speaking into the intercom.

Reluctantly I got the phone out of my backpack, afraid he might take it away from me. But all he did was look for a moment. "He have phone," he said into the intercom. "I see it."

The buzzer came on and we pushed open the inner door, just in time—she'd barely left it on for a second. There was no elevator, so we had to walk up to the fourth floor. After we knocked on her door a long time passed while we listened to the sounds of bolts being pulled and locks being unlocked. Finally the door opened a crack and a dark eye peeked out. "He didn't tell me he had that long hair," Lola's voice said, not approvingly.

I was tired of people criticizing my hair. "Long hair isn't going to hurt you," I couldn't keep from saying, then felt bad about it—maybe she had good reason to be so scared.

Finally the door opened. "Hurry!" Lola said in an urgent whisper, and rushed us in so quickly I barely had a chance to look at her. Then she was locking the locks and bolting the bolts shut again.

She had on black pants and a black top and her hair was plain and black and unstylish, and she wore no makeup. She might have been good-looking if she weren't so thin and bedraggled—was she too nervous to eat? And her skin was pale and her eyes red from crying. She seemed completely wretched, and you could tell it was not her imagination that was doing this to her. Finally she turned and looked at Trang. "He showed you the phone? The same one you had?"

"I tell you that," Trang said

"Hello, Nick," she said to me, and held out her hand. I took it carefully, not wanting to be the least bit rough with her, she seemed so fragile. She was shorter than I was, and made a sad attempt to smile politely. "Come in. Sit down," she said.

The furniture was shabby and worn, and it was all black. The old carpeting was dark gray. A few black-and-white prints leaned against the walls, and a mirror, and there were boxes around, as though she had just moved in. Opened suitcases, too. "Is this a new place?" I asked her.

"No." She sighed. "I just never had the chance—or the money—to fix it up the way I'd like. If you can't go out, it's hard to earn money." She sat down on a black chair and we sat on a black couch across from her. Between us was a black metal coffee table with a black ceramic vase on it.

"Why can't you ever go out? Why do you have so many locks?" I couldn't help asking her.

"That's the way you have to live if your life is in danger," she said, twisting her hands together. "That's why I need all the help I can get. You look like a wiry young guy. I'm lucky you bought that phone." She gulped. "Did Fleck call you again?"

Trang was watching me now too. What was I supposed to say? He would know if I was lying. I didn't like lying, especially not in front of someone who knew. But weren't we both already lying to her by not telling her Fleck was waiting outside in the car?

"He called me, but . . . he can't seem to get out of wherever he is."

She gave me a hard look. Could she tell I was lying?

"But what difference does it make about Fleck anyway?" I asked her. And then I dared to add, "He's not the one you're in danger from—at least that's the feeling I'm getting."

"No, he's not," she admitted. At last somebody was giving me some answers! She smiled wanly. "I'm so sorry to trouble you, I know this isn't your problem. But you have the phone, and whoever has the phone is in touch with Fleck, and Fleck might be able to save me from the person I'm in danger from, if he's willing. If and when Fleck gets out—and he's clever enough to get out of anywhere—then maybe I'll be in even more danger, or maybe you can convince him to help me. You're the only one in a position to do that. That's why I'm depending on you."

Who could I believe, Fleck or Lola? There was no reason not to tell her that he said he wanted to help her—she knew I was in touch with him through the phone. "Fleck keeps saying he wants to save you from this other person, but that you're too afraid of him."

Two tears rolled down her cheeks. "It . . . it doesn't matter what he says. He hates me. He thinks I'm the one who killed him. They all do. Oh, if only they knew!" She buried her head in her hands, sobbing.

I felt sorry for her, but I had heard her cry so much that it no longer had much effect on me. And she kept switching back and forth from thinking Fleck could help her and thinking he never would. "He never told me he thinks you killed him," I said. "He said he wanted to help you—and that you're in danger from somebody else. So did you. Who is it you're so afraid of, then?"

She wiped her eyes and sat up straight again. "I don't know if I'm at liberty to say," she said primly.

I sighed. "How can I help you if nobody will tell me anything?" I wanted to know.

She swallowed, and wiped away another tear. "Rusty's going to kill me, because Fleck and I were the only ones between him and our grandfather's fortune. Rusty was only ten years old when he killed

Fleck. That's why everybody still thinks it was me. They all dote on Rusty and could never believe he would do something like that. But I was there. I saw the look on his face when he left his roller skates right at the top of the stairs of grandpa's house. Fleck had gone upstairs to have another secret drink and that's when Rusty put the skates in exactly the right place so that Fleck slipped on the skates and went all the way down the stairs and broke his neck. It looked like an accident, which is the only reason I didn't get legally accused, but the whole family hates me now." She twisted her fingers. "And for the last eight years I've been the only one between Rusty and his fortune. And Rusty knows it. Oh, how he knows it!"

She sighed deeply and shook her head. "Rusty killed Fleck eight years ago and I've been hiding from Rusty ever since. I know he's going to kill me soon because in a few weeks he's going to turn eighteen, and that's when the money would come to him if it weren't for me. And it would be too obvious if he did it right before his eighteenth birthday." She was fighting hard not to cry again now. "Do you know what it feels like to be a prisoner in your own home? Not home. Series of temporary homes." She shook her head, smiling sadly again. "I can *feel* you're a good-hearted young man—I felt it as soon as you answered the phone. The police and all the other authorities won't believe me that Rusty wants me dead because nobody else in the family will talk about the will—it's a closely guarded secret. They all want Rusty to get it because he's more like the rest of the family than I am—more popular, more outgoing, more conventional—their redheaded boy wonder. So of course he's only attracted to red-headed girls—it's a form of self-love. He can have children and I can't. Plus, they think I killed Fleck and don't believe Rusty did it. Fleck thinks so, too. I'm the outsider. With Rusty, the money will stay in the family. And because of all the secrecy, the police won't believe me. They think I'm being hysterical."

She sure *sounded* hysterical. "But how could Fleck call me if he died eight years ago?" I asked her, acting ignorant.

Her face went even paler. "He's . . . he's calling you from hell," she whispered, then buried her head in her hands, shaking her head and whimpering.

I looked over at Trang sitting next to me, chewing on his nails and watching Lola, refusing to look back at me. "And he was calling you from hell, before you returned the phone?" I asked him. "But it looks like a new phone. So how did he find out the number if he's been there for eight years?"

He shook his head and shrugged. He wasn't smoking; probably Lola didn't allow it in her apartment. "I don't know. He very clever. Then he try to make me get him out, and I return it."

"They let people make phone calls to us from hell?" I asked him. "How could he do that? And how could a phone get him out?" This was sounding fishy again now. Though, on the other hand, the way Fleck looked and smelled, he really could have come from hell. The idea *had* come to me on my own. And the phone sure had acted weird when I put those attachments on it and did what he told me.

I still didn't know what to believe.

"Ask him," Trang said, and then, remembering that Fleck didn't want Lola to know he was around, he said, "Next time he call you, I mean. I think, that only number he can call."

Lola lifted her head from her hands and looked at me pleadingly. "Nick? Nick? Rusty's crazy. He's a psychopath. Please save me from him. You're the only one who can. Because you have the phone."

"What does the phone have to do with it?" I said, thoroughly confused now.

"Because you're in touch with Fleck. And Rusty *has* to be afraid of Fleck, because he killed him. If Rusty's scared, he might not try to kill me. He already has plenty of money."

"Wait a minute." I stood up. "This Rusty person is going to believe that someone who died eight years ago is a threat to him? You expect me to tell him something crazy like that? I don't even know the guy!"

Now Lola seemed confused. She coughed and put her hand to her mouth. "Oh. That's right. You don't know him. But at least maybe you can convince Fleck, when he calls you. He said he wanted to help me? That's how he can help me. Tell him Rusty killed him, not me. He may believe it. Rusty Girard. He's the only one in the phone book. He's a monster. He has been since he was born. Remind Fleck of that and maybe he'll believe you. And then . . . maybe Fleck *will* decide to try to help me. That's why I need you. Please?"

"Okay. I'll do what I can, when he calls," I said, heading for the door. This whole thing was freaking me out even more now, for some reason I didn't understand. "I have to get home now. My girlfriend's waiting. I'll see what I can tell Fleck. If he calls me again."

"He will call," Trang said. "That only number he can call."

"Please, Nick," Lola called after me as we headed down the stairs. "Try to convince Fleck to help me. He's a jerk, but not a psychopath like Rusty."

I was more eager than ever to get back home now.

Fleck grinned at us when we got into the car. "So how's my darling Lola?" he said.

I shook my head. "I think you're all crazy," I said. "She thinks you believe she killed you, and that's why she's afraid of you. Is that what you believe?"

"That's what the family believes," he said. "But I happen to know it was that little monster Rusty. And he'll kill again. He'd kill just for the sheer *fun* of it, never mind the fortune."

"Like I said, you're *all* insane," I told him. "And it doesn't have anything to do with me. I'm not a part of your crazy family. Take me home now. I've got to see Jen."

Before I turned back to the front to keep my eyes on Trang's driving, Fleck flashed me a funny, ironic smile that I couldn't decipher.

Trang didn't even check the street as he began to pull the car out of the parking place. Luckily I did. "Stop!" I shouted, as a car whizzed past. If I hadn't done that, it would have rammed right into us. "Don't you even know to *look?*" I screamed at him.

"Sorry," he said, as he jerked forward.

"Is it true what she said?" I asked Fleck. "You died because this Rusty person left his roller skates at the top of the stairs?"

"The little monster knew what he was doing even at the age of ten. That's when he found out about the will. Lola and I were in the way. Now it's only Lola. She's been in hiding ever since, running from place to place. But she can't go on like this forever. And you were unlucky enough to buy Trang's phone, the only number I could wangle in hell. Lola believes in things like destiny. I bet she thinks you and I can somehow stop Rusty from killing her."

"Tell me about it," I said. "Hey, there's a stop sign on this corner!"

I saved our lives for the second time. I considered just getting out of the car and walking home. But I took the risk of riding with Trang because I wanted to talk to Jen as soon as possible. And I still wanted some answers. I turned back to Fleck. "But how could a phone get you out of hell? Bring you back to life?"

"They're slobs down there, but they know a lot of stuff that we don't know. Future technology, for instance. They like to taunt us with it because we can't have it there. But I've always been a computer whiz. I put two and two together and figured out what you could do with equipment from today. I wasn't one hundred percent sure it would work, but here I am!" He smiled brightly at me.

Could I believe him? It still sounded absurd, despite everything I had seen. I was starting to think about giving the phone to the police again. If I got rid of it, the Callers couldn't reach me.

Then my stomach sank. I could never get rid of them. Fleck and Trang knew where I lived. I'd had to tell Trang so I could get Fleck out of my house. So Lola as good as knew, too. There was no way I could get rid of them. If *only* I had never bought this phone! If *only* I had never followed Fleck's instructions! How could I be so stupid? How was I ever going to get out of this mess?

"Poor lady," Trang said softly. "Eight years, hiding. Never go out."

"She must be wildly in debt, too," Fleck said, clucking. "She's too afraid to touch the family money, because then Rusty could find her. She has to do piecework at home. Trang's her middleman. Rusty doesn't know about him."

"How do you know anything about her life? You died as soon as this kid found out about the will."

"I've been talking to Trang, remember? He filled me in on the situation."

"But how did you find out his number? They didn't have phones like that eight years ago. And why did they let you make phone calls to the earth from hell, anyway?"

"Ever hear the word corruption? There's plenty of it down there, of course—they invented it. You can find out information, get a few privileges, if you go in for some extra torture. Not everybody down there is in as bad shape as I am. Of course many are a lot worse."

We turned into the trailer park. Now I could relax a little. I'd get rid of the phone tomorrow. And then I'd figure out some way to keep these three nuts out of my life. I'd tell the cops everything if I had to.

Not that the cops would ever believe me, not with how crazy the whole story was.

"See you later, Nicky," Fleck said, laughing, as I got out of the car.

I slammed the car door and stomped into the house.

I would use the phone one last time, to call Jen

and find out what was with this guy with the car. And then I'd turn it off and never turn it on again.

As soon as I got into the trailer I locked the door behind me and got the phone out and turned it on. I called Jen fast, before any of them could call me. For once Jen answered, not her mother.

"Nick!" she said. "I'm glad you called. Sorry my dad was so harsh with you last night."

"Did your mother tell you I called again this morning?" I was sort of nervous about bringing it up now, she sounded perfectly normal, but I knew I had to get it out in the open. "She said . . . she said you were out with a guy from another school. With a new car."

"Oh. Yeah, I told her I met him when we had a game at his school. Actually, I don't remember meeting him. He called me last night. He's a senior and came to our school for a wrestling meet, and remembered seeing me, and asked around about me, and found out who I was, and asked me to go out for a drive. And it was such a nice day. But don't worry, Nick. Rusty was just a way to kill time when I couldn't find you."

"Rusty?" I said, feeling cold.

"Rusty Girard. He's nice, but nothing like you. I'll tell you all about it."

Rusty Girard.

Lola had said there was only one Rusty Girard in the phone book. Could this one possibly be the same person she was afraid was going to kill her? A psychopath? And today he had taken Jen out in his new car. How could such a coincidence happen?

"When he was born they named him Russell," Jen was saying. "But he had it legally changed to Rusty. That's what everybody calls him, because of his hair. But it's not as nice as your hair."

I was barely listening to her. Was it really the same person?

"I mean it's even a little bit thin. Yours is so much thicker."

"Does he know about you and me?" I couldn't stop myself from asking her.

"Of course." She almost sounded a little irritated. "You think I wouldn't tell him I was already going out with you? Not that he was interested in hearing very much about you. You can hardly blame him."

And if this *was* the same person Lola and Fleck had been talking about, how had he found Jen? Lola had said Rusty liked red-headed girls. Was it just a coincidence that he had run into Jen? It couldn't be.

Had somebody—such as Fleck or Lola—told him about her?

"Nick? Nick? Why aren't you saying anything?"

"Er . . ." What could I tell her? "Does he have a nice car?"

"A red convertible sports car. If I knew more about cars I could tell you the name. It was nice with the top down."

I thought about my old bike, and how I had been riding around in Trang's reeking old wreck while she had been in this fancy convertible with the top down. Again, I couldn't stop myself. "He must be loaded. Not like me. Your mother said he was a fine young man."

"Oh, you know what *she's* like. She just said that

because money impresses her. I don't think 'fine' is the right word for him. He was interesting, though."

"Interesting?"

"Nick! You're not jealous, are you? It's not like that. Why don't you come over? My parents are at some event that's going to go on all day."

I still had a lot of homework. I'd been too busy with the Callers to even think about it. But this was more important. I hadn't seen Jen since Friday night, and then I'd been preoccupied with the phone—the phone that seemed to be wrecking my life.

"I'd like to come. But I can't stay very long. I've got a lot of homework. And you know I have to do it all by hand." The second I'd said that I wished I hadn't. I didn't want to rub it in how poor I was compared to this Rusty person.

"You could use my computer. I'm all done with my stuff."

"I'd rather spend the time with you. But maybe I'll bring some of it. We can see what happens."

"Okay. Come over right away. See you."

"I'll leave now. Bye."

I hung up the phone and turned it off immediately. I didn't want any of them calling me. And yet for some reason I made sure to take the phone with me, along with some books and assignments.

And before I left—I couldn't stop myself—I looked up Girard in the phone book. Lola had been right, there was only one Rusty Girard. The address was 1 Brussels Place, which sounded fancy, and of course had to be a house since there was no apartment number. If he was about to turn eighteen—Lola had said it was eight years since he had killed Fleck at the age of ten—then presumably he still lived with his parents, who must be the Adele and Fred Girard who were also listed at the same address with a different phone number.

As I rode over to Jen's I tried not to resent this guy, but I couldn't help it. He had everything I didn't have. I was sure he didn't have to work. If he had a car like that, it meant his parents could afford to send him to any college—he didn't have to hope for a scholarship the way I did. And anyway, in a few weeks he was going to inherit a fortune that was enough to risk killing for.

Once he got rid of pathetic Lola, that is, who had been hiding from him in her crummy apartments for eight years. I wondered how he was going to do it—and if it was possible to stop him somehow.

"Don't think about it," I said out loud, pedaling furiously. Jen would make everything all right. I trusted her.

When I pulled up to Jen's, a sleek red Fiat convertible was parked in front of her house.

I felt a flicker of panic as well as anger. Should I go in? Or wait outside?

No. I wouldn't back down so easily. And I couldn't help being curious. If this guy had a speck of decency he'd leave soon after I got there.

But maybe he didn't have a speck of decency. Fleck and Lola had both said he was a monster.

How had he found out about Jen, anyway? That question kept bothering me.

I parked the bike where I always did and went around to the front door and rang the bell.

Jen answered, looking a little confused. Her red hair, which was usually neatly combed—except when she was playing soccer—was tousled. Why? From the ride in the convertible? Or for some other reason?

"Did that Rusty guy come back?" I whispered.

"He couldn't find his Swiss Army knife," she whispered back. "He thought he might have accidentally left it here when he came in to meet my parents."

Of course he would have a Swiss Army knife,

probably one of the fanciest ones with a million blades and parts on it. Of course I could never afford anything like that. And why would he have left a knife here?

"Come on in, Nick," Jen said in a normal voice. "I told Rusty you were about to come over."

A guy around my own age was poking around the pillows on the living room couch. He was taller than me, and looked well built. He had a cleft chin and blue eyes and, of course, red hair. It wasn't thin, like Jen had said. A lock of it hung down over his forehead, like somebody in the movies, and he kept pushing it back.

He looked up when we entered the room. "Rusty, this is Nick. Nick, this is Rusty," Jen said.

He smiled at me, an open, friendly smile, and stood up straight and came around the couch and held out his right hand. "Hi, Nick. Nice to meet you," he said.

What could I do? "Nice to meet you, Rusty," I said, and we shook hands. I noticed that he was wearing a very fancy watch. His clothes were all new and expensive. His hair looked casual but you could tell he went to a hairstylist—the way it kept just falling over one eye was too perfect.

He scratched his head. "I was sure I had that knife when I came over here this morning," he said, looking puzzled. He shrugged. "Well, this is where I sat. I didn't go anywhere else in the house. I'll have to check the car again. Anyway, I can always get another one." He looked at his fancy watch. "Well, I've got to get back. Thanks for a nice time, Jen," he said, and then he actually leaned toward her and kissed her on the cheek. He grinned at me. "Nice to meet you, Nick. Hope we run into each other again. You have really great hair. I wish mine was that thick."

He was the only person I had met since getting the phone who hadn't criticized my hair. But it didn't make me like him any better.

Jen saw him to the door. As soon as he was gone I said, "Was that kiss really necessary?"

Jen frowned. "He just kissed me on the cheek. Like a friend," she said.

"Was it the first time he kissed you?"

Her frown deepened. "What's gotten into you, Nick? You've never been like this before. Jealous, I mean. There's nothing going on with him. You and I never lie to each other. Or do we? I could ask you where *you* were last night and all day today."

I couldn't believe it. We had never had even this

much of an argument before—except about the phone. And why had this Rusty person come along right after I got the phone? Had he really just seen her at some meet and found out how to reach her? It was a pretty unbelievable coincidence, especially since he really did seem to be the person Lola was so afraid of.

On the surface Rusty seemed perfectly nice, but that didn't mean anything about what he was really like. And I didn't like the way he had kissed Jen in front of me.

How had he really found her? I was pretty sure Fleck had to have connected them somehow.

Meanwhile, what was I going to tell her about where I had been today? She already didn't like the phone, she wanted me to turn it in. I had told her about this threatening guy Fleck. What would she think if I told her I had brought him here, seemingly from hell, and that now he knew where I lived?

She had also reminded me that we never lied to each other, and as far as I knew we didn't. But how could I tell her the truth, especially about Rusty, and Lola being afraid he was going to kill her? The phone was just making everything worse and worse.

"I worked an extra shift today," I said. "Because of

spending the money on the phone. I wish I'd never bought the stupid thing." That, at least, was the truth. But I had still told her the first lie since I'd met her. I hated that. But I didn't know what else to do.

"But what about that woman who cries all the time?" Jen was saying. "I thought you were worried about her and wanted to help her."

What was I going to say? That Lola was afraid Jen's new friend was going to kill her?

I was still wearing my backpack. From inside it, the phone mewed. But I was sure I had turned it off. Was it driving me nuts, or what?

"You brought that thing with you?" Jen said, not pleasantly.

"I'm afraid of what would happen if it rang when my Mom was home," I said, shrugging off the backpack and unzipping it. I pulled it out and turned it off without answering it. "I was sure I turned it off. It would have been a disaster if Mom found it."

"Well, at least I'm glad you're not answering it anymore." She peered closer. "What are those attachments? The phone didn't have them before. Why did you get them? And how?"

The house phone rang and she went to answer it.

I quickly dropped the cell phone back into the backpack, hoping she'd forget about the attachments.

"Oh, hi, Rusty," Jen said, giving me an odd look. "You just left a couple of minutes ago . . . Oh, yeah, I'm glad you found it. But, um, why is a *knife* so important to you? . . . Oh, I see . . . What?" She bit her lip. "Saturday?" She sighed. "But Rusty, I told you. Nick and I are going out. I can't just . . . No, we're not *engaged.* Listen, I think it might be better if you didn't call me again, okay? . . . What? Longfellow House? No, I've never been there." There was something wistful about the way she said that. Then her mouth hardened. "Look, I'm busy right now. I can't talk about it. Okay? Bye." She slowly put the phone down.

"Longfellow House?" I said. It was the fanciest and most expensive country club and restaurant in town.

"You heard what I said." Her tone was defensive. "That I'm going out with you and I don't want him calling me again."

"Yeah, but I bet you'd love going to Longfellow House." I couldn't help it. Who *wouldn't* want to go there? And I could never take her in a million years.

"Look, you and I are a couple, okay? I told him that. He's just being pushy." But she didn't sound very convincing.

"It's true that you've never been there, isn't it. This is your big chance," I said, and I was aware of the anger in my voice. Even her parents didn't have the kind of money to casually go to Longfellow House.

"Let's just forget about it, okay?" she said, sounding angry too.

I was hurting inside like I never had before. Jen was the most important person in my life. How could this be happening? And what a jerk this Rusty guy was to call her and ask her out when he knew I was right here in her house.

Could Lola and Fleck be right about him being a psychopath? I had to find out before things with Jen got any worse. Had Fleck known Rusty was the kind of person who would immediately start trying to date Jen, even though she already had a boyfriend? I bet he had.

I forced myself to smile at her. It wasn't easy for me and I didn't know how real it looked. "I'm sorry," I said. I walked over and kissed her on the mouth. I pulled away and said, "It's just that . . . you know how I feel about you."

"And you know how I feel about you. It doesn't matter that he has all that money."

It had finally been mentioned directly. Then I remembered something. "You said you didn't think 'fine' was the right word for him. But that he was interesting. What did you mean by that?"

She frowned again, as though I were prying, but she quickly covered it up. "Well, he's always polite, like to my parents and to you. But when you're with him he has this sort of nasty sense of humor." I immediately thought of Fleck. As different as they were, they were relatives, and might have some things in common. "I mean he sort of puts people down a lot. It was a feeling like he and I were the cool ones, and almost everybody else was beneath us somehow."

Again, the words came out without me thinking about them. "It wasn't that polite of him to call and ask you out when he knew I was here. And I'm sure he would think of me as being way beneath him, with no money and just an old bike."

"He said he liked your hair!" she almost snapped at me.

Was she defending him? I forced myself to be realistic instead of emotional. He was a dangerous topic. The best thing would be to change the subject. I could find out more about him later. Such as if he really was the relative of Fleck and Lola who would get a fortune if Lola died. And if he really was a monster. I thought of the knife again.

We sat on her couch for awhile. She was as affectionate as ever. But now she said she wasn't sure when her parents were coming home, so we didn't go very far. Before she had said they would be away all day. Why had she changed her mind about that?

So I did some of my homework on her computer, while she watched TV. It was unusual to be in the same place and yet not be together. Were things with her changing? Was it because of Rusty?

The phone rang and I could hear her talking in the living room. It was Rusty. He seemed to be pushing her to go to the Longfellow House with him again. It made me so furious I stopped being able to concentrate. Now he really was being obnoxious. And yet Jen didn't hang up immediately, even though she kept saying she couldn't go. What would she have said if I hadn't been there?

I turned off the computer and gathered up my books and papers and put them in the backpack. I couldn't stand to stay here and listen to this. I knew it wasn't fair to blame Jen, it wasn't her fault this pushy rich kid was bothering her. But that didn't mean I had to listen to it.

As soon as she got off the phone I put on the backpack and went back into the living room. "I think I better go," I said. "Your parents might come home at any time." I shrugged. "And to be honest, it's hard for me to concentrate with him calling you all the time."

"I keep telling him I'm not going out with him!" she snapped. "What else am I supposed to do? Have the phone disconnected?"

"I think you should be careful of that guy," I said. "I have reason to believe he might be . . . dangerous."

"You *are* jealous!" she accused me. "How can you know anything about him?"

"Because of . . . of the phone." I didn't know what else to say.

"Your stupid phone again? That doesn't make any sense."

"Just be careful, Jen," I said, and kissed her quickly, and left. And all the way home I knew what they meant when they talked about having a heavy heart.

Almost as soon as I got home, the phone mewed again.

It didn't have caller ID. And now it seemed you couldn't turn it off. It was changing. Getting worse.

Now the phone had become something different. I *had* to answer it because I couldn't turn it off. That made everything harder.

Luckily Mom was away from home most of the time at her jobs. At night I would have to sleep with the phone under my pillow, to prevent her from hearing it if it rang, and so I could answer it fast.

Would it be possible to ask them not to call me during school or work hours, or when Mom was at home?

Anyway, Mom wasn't home now, and I couldn't stand to listen to it mewing and mewing. I pressed the green button. "Hello?"

"Oh, Nick, I'm so glad you answered," Lola said, her voice tearful with gratitude. "I so much wanted to apologize to you. I hope I didn't scare you away—or make you want to throw away the phone."

Pathetic as she was, I knew I had to be honest with her—the situation was too critical for me to be fooling around. "Well, I have to say, I don't really know what to think about all this."

"I won't bug you about it anymore. I just don't want to scare you away. I still need to know the person with the phone."

I was about to tell her that I was going to get rid of the phone tomorrow anyway. But then I knew I *wasn't* going to get rid of it.

But I wasn't ready yet to tell Lola I had met Rusty.

"Why do you need to know the person with the phone? What *is* it about this phone, anyway?" I asked Lola.

"It's the only way I can find out about Fleck. Like, if he ever escapes from hell or anything."

"Well, I've got to tell you something else about this phone," I said. "It not only doesn't have caller ID, now I can't turn it off. I don't like that. It's dangerous—for you as well as for me. If my mother ever hears it I'm completely sunk. If I brought it to school and to work, so she wouldn't hear it, and it rang, I'd be in trouble. And I can't afford to get in trouble at school or work because I have to get a scholarship to college." I was about to add "unlike Rusty," but managed to stop myself. "So I'm going to have to ask you only to call me at certain times. Otherwise I have to get rid of it, for sure."

"Just tell me. I promise, I promise. Please, Nick. I'll do whatever you say. Just don't get rid of the phone."

So I told her when she could call me and when she couldn't. Not during school or work hours, not late at night when Mom got home, and not on Friday and Saturday evenings when I would be with Jen. That still left a lot of free time on weekday evenings when she could call me. She agreed, eagerly, promising over and over again. She just needed to know that she could reach me.

"If you told me *your* phone number, then I could call when it was convenient for me," I suggested. "You're always at home anyway."

"Oh, no, I can't do that!" she said, sounding horrified. "What if Rusty found out my number?"

"Why would I tell him? I don't even know him. If you want to be in touch with me, it would be so much easier if I could call you."

She didn't want to admit that. "I promise I'll only

call at the times you said. Thank you, thank you, for not throwing it away. I so desperately need your help." And she hung up.

I was trying to concentrate on my homework, with difficulty, when it rang again fifteen minutes later. I had no choice but to answer it.

"Well, as you'd expect, Trang lives in a real dump," Fleck said. "But it's still a palace compared to where I was for the last eight years. Of course, there's a big problem with money. Trang hardly has enough to get by himself, and I can't get any kind of job until my appearance gets more . . . er, acceptable."

"Why are you telling *me* your money problems? You know I don't have any money. Don't even *think* about borrowing from me."

"If only I could borrow some from Rusty. He's loaded, even though he's desperate enough to kill to get even more. Maybe you could get some from him." He laughed.

I was dumbstruck. *Had* he told Rusty about Jen? I wasn't going to admit yet that I'd met him, that was for sure. "How could I try to borrow money from Rusty if I don't even know him? Anyway, you said he was a monster. Monsters don't lend people money fairly, no matter how rich they are."

"You may not know him yourself, but your precious girlfriend does by now. What did *she* think of him? I bet he blew her mind." He chuckled his wicked chuckle.

Was it possible? The first night Fleck had arrived, when I had left him alone with the phone for a minute or two, could he have made the call connecting Rusty with Jen? The only number I had called on the phone was Jen's. The phone didn't seem to have many normal funtions but it could remember numbers.

"Did you give Rusty her number? Did you? But why? You—you—" I couldn't think of a bad enough word.

"Hold on, hold on, pal!" It was the first time I'd heard Fleck sound afraid. "I wouldn't do that. Why would I put your precious girlfriend in danger from that psycho? It must have been the phone."

"The phone? How could the phone have anything to do with it? I don't know what you're talking about."

"Haven't you noticed?" he asked me. "That phone has a mind of its own. And it's more than just a phone now."

In a weird way, he was making a certain kind of sense. Jen's face had spontaneously, impossibly appeared on it, and a picture of Jen in a torture machine. If the phone could do that, then what was to stop it from somehow giving her number to Rusty? If I could believe it got out Fleck out of hell, I could believe that.

"I'll think about it," I said. Automatically I started to hang up so I could turn off the phone and end this conversation. Then I remembered that I couldn't turn it off—and that I also had to try to get him to agree only to call me at certain times. I was so mad at him I didn't know if I could control myself enough to sound rational. But I had to get that promise out of him. If it was possible to get any kind of promise out of someone like Fleck.

"Now listen good," I said. "This . . . this *phone* that I ended up with—and I believe you that it's more than just a phone—got even worse now. I can't turn it off. There are a lot of times when it will screw up my life completely if it rings. And I swear, I will have it destroyed tomorrow unless you promise to call only at certain times."

He must have been able to hear the absolute determination in my voice. "Okay, okay, just tell me when," he said, not joking or being sarcastic anymore.

I told him. And he seemed to promise, in a serious way, to go along with it. I hoped I could believe him.

I also hoped I could believe that he hadn't told Rusty about Jen. "Well, if the phone somehow told Rusty about Jen, that story about him seeing her at a meet was a lie. The first thing he said to her was a lie."

"So you're beginning to see that Lola and I are right about him."

Obnoxious as Fleck was, there was nobody else I could talk to about this. I told him everything that had happened with Rusty at Jen's today.

"That's just like him, pestering her to go out with him in front of you. I promise you, to know him is to hate him. Lola's an angel in comparison. And that's why . . ." He paused. "That's why I've got to stop him from hurting her."

"Stop him? How? What are you talking about?"

"Stop him . . . for good," Fleck said. And the way he said it actually made me shiver.

"Wait a minute . . ." I said.

"I mean doing to him what he did to me," Fleck said. "Fair's fair, after all."

"But then you'd just end up in hell all over again!" I protested. I didn't like Rusty, but I didn't want to know somebody who was actually going to kill him.

"Don't you remember what I said? I'd be killing

Rusty to help Lola, to save her. She wants him dead, too . . . You know she does. And maybe saving Jen, too, if she starts hanging out with him. Anybody who knows him is in danger. And if what you're doing is to help somebody, then you don't get sent to hell. I haven't decided what I'll do yet. I'll let you know when I do, chum."

"I don't want to hear about it," I said, and I really didn't. I wondered what had gotten him into hell in the first place. "Anyway, I'm busy. I've got to go."

"You're doing your precious homework, right? Well, get back to it." He hung up.

Amazingly, the Callers kept their promise. They never called me at a time when it would get me in trouble.

Meanwhile, Jen told me at school that she had accepted Rusty's invitation. I was horrified, but I knew arguing with her about him would be a big mistake. I had to play it cool. I just shrugged and said, "Fine. I can understand why you'd want to go to Longfellow House."

She took my hand. "Thanks for being so great about it, Nick."

We didn't say anything else about it, but it was

there on both of our minds. I was also aware that she wasn't asking me if I had gotten rid of the phone, and I wasn't telling her anything about it. Suddenly there were these two major things that we weren't talking about. We still hung out together, but now there were longer silences than there had been before. It was awful.

Saturday night and the date with Rusty were getting closer every day. But because I was trying not to act jealous, I was hoping she'd tell me what happened on their date. And if Rusty was the kind of person he had seemed to be at first, then I couldn't believe she could like him, or want to go out with him ever again. I would wait until I found out what happened on Saturday to tell her it could be dangerous for her to get to know him any better By then, maybe she would trust me enough to listen.

On Saturday night, at home alone, I tried to concentrate on homework. It was harder than it had ever been. I was almost hoping one of the others would call me, just to distract me—though I wasn't sure what I would tell Lola, since she still didn't know that Fleck was back or that I had met Rusty, and I didn't want her to know. If she knew, she might try to persuade me to get involved with Fleck's plan to murder him.

As it got later I was hoping Jen would call me when she got home. She knew Mom worked late on Saturdays. But I stayed up, and no call came. When I finally went to bed, sleep was almost impossible. As I lay there in the dark, I decided I wouldn't call her in the morning. I would wait to see if she called me. If I called first it might seem as if I was jealous, and she wouldn't believe anything I had to say.

On Sunday morning I waited and waited. She didn't call. Finally, at one in the afternoon, I couldn't stand it anymore, and called her. "Oh, hi, Nick," she said. "What's up?"

Of course she knew I wanted to find out what her date with Rusty had been like. Was she trying to avoid telling me? "Uh . . . how was Longfellow House?" I said, feeling completely pitiful.

"It was okay," she said evasively, not offering any details, such as what it was like inside, what they ate, how expensive it was.

But there was one thing I couldn't stop myself from asking her about. "How was Rusty? I mean . . . did he, uh, try anything?"

"Well, afterward he was kind of pushy. You know what he was like, about asking me out. He said he was going to come into a lot of money really soon. As if that would make a difference. It's a good thing I'm strong from playing soccer."

It was obvious that he'd made a pass at her and she'd had to fight him off. But she wasn't really telling me about it, the way she normally would have. She was just hinting. That wasn't like her.

Did that mean she had *liked* him? Had she really fought him off? Or had she gone along with it? There was no way I could find out without really being pathetic.

I was hurt, but I was also boiling. The guy was worse than I had imagined. And I was scared for her. She didn't know he was a psycho. She would probably take it the wrong way, given the strange mood she was in. But I cared about her, and I had to try to protect her. "Jen, I'm worried about you. You better stay away from this guy. You understand? I'm not jealous, I'm worried." I wanted to tell her where all this money was going to come from—from the death, of a woman who had been hiding in terror from him for eight years. That Rusty had already killed somebody else who was in the way of him getting the money. But of course I couldn't tell her about that because she'd want to know how I knew. I couldn't tell Jen anything I had learned about Rusty from the Callers.

"Oh, Nick, don't be so hysterical," she said. "I mean, sure, he's full of himself and a little pushy. But he's not going to hurt me or anything." She said it as though I were overreacting, as though I were somebody like Lola. "Anyway, I have to go. See you." And she hung up.

She had never hung up on me before.

I put down the receiver, feeling a terrible mixture of emotions. The best thing would be if Rusty just laid off, and forgot about Jen. Lola and Fleck were right. He sure seemed like a dangerous psychopath. How could he just move in on somebody else's girlfriend? And that wasn't the worst thing he had done, by far.

But what if he didn't lay off? What if he didn't forget about Jen? What if she dropped me for him? I had never imagined that could happen. But the way she sounded today, it seemed really possible.

What Fleck said he was going to do to Rusty was still unthinkable.

But not as unthinkable as before.

12

The next day Jen ate lunch with a bunch of girls from the soccer team whom I didn't know. It was the first time we hadn't had lunch together since we started going out. After school she had soccer practice. We didn't have a chance to talk to each other once all day. I was miserable, but I did everything I could to hide it.

Was this really happening? Was Jen actually going to drop me for that jerk? Did she really care about superficial things, like how rich he was, how good-looking, his big muscles? How could he have that power over her? And what did he ultimately have in mind? I was as worried about her as I was miserable for myself.

"I can just tell Rusty's going to move soon," Lola

said on the phone. "I can feel it." She was crying, as usual. "His birthday's getting closer. I'm so scared. Do you realize I've been in hiding since I was twenty? And now I'm twenty-eight. My twenties are gone and I'll never live to thirty."

I wanted to tell her I was almost as scared of him as she was, but I still managed not to let that out. It seemed as if the more I told the Callers, the more they sucked me into their mad world. "I wish I could help you," I said to Lola. "But I . . . I just . . ."

She just kept crying.

"Rusty picked Jen up after soccer practice today," Fleck told me later in the week.

"How do you know?"

"I sent Trang to check on her. Rusty was driving so fast with Jen that even Trang had a problem keeping up with him—and you know how fast *he* drives. And then they went and— Well, maybe I shouldn't tell you."

"Tell me!" I demanded.

"They parked on Highland Drive." Highland Drive was a notorious make-out place. "Don't worry, it was broad daylight and they were in his open convertible," he reassured me, and then added, "Rusty showed her tricks he can do with his precious knife."

I didn't say anything. I was scared for her—and furious at Rusty.

"Trang is worried about you," Fleck said. "He understands what it's like to lose someone you love—he had to leave his wife behind in Vietnam, and he loved her more than anything. I can bet you all those Vietnamese songs on the phone are about losing the person you love."

"What makes you so sure I've lost her already?" I demanded.

Now he didn't say anything.

My grades were going down. I was getting hardly any sleep. I drowsed at school and at work. I just barely managed not to spill the fifty-gallon milk tank. When I saw Jen, she looked like she was losing weight. The phone was ruining my life. And yet I took it everywhere with me, terrified that it would ring.

The worst of it was that I kept thinking about what was happening to Jen, and to me, and what had already happened to Lola, all because of Rusty. I was beginning to be obsessed with him.

I got a friend to help me find his e-mail address on a computer at school. He didn't just have an e-mail address, the jerk had his own Web site—a fancy one, with lots of pictures and links. It was all about what a great athlete he was, the trophies he had won for sports and body building, pictures of him posing in briefs at competitions, his muscles gleaming with oil, a smug grin on his face, his hair still cutely falling down his forehead. There were also pictures of important social functions of his prominent family, Rusty in tuxedos, with women in evening gowns. There was never any mention of Lola or Fleck, even though they were part of the same family. Only Rusty, Rusty, Rusty. It made me sick. But I kept looking at it. And my grades kept going down.

I cornered Jen at her locker after school one day a week or so later. "Jen, what's going on?" I asked her. We both looked tired and ragged. "Are you really dropping me for him? Because he's rich?"

For a moment she looked at me in a pleading way, and suddenly I felt sorry for her. Then her eyes shifted away. "Just . . . just leave it be, for the time being," she said in a dull voice. "It'll be better that way. For both of us."

I grabbed her arm. "Are you . . . are you scared of him? Is *that* why you're going around with him?"

"He makes threats about you," she said, still not

meeting my eyes. "Don't try anything. Don't interfere. I've got to go. He's waiting for me." She hurried away.

Unlike Lola, Fleck had no problem giving out his phone number. And one day I called him at Trang's and said, "You got any ideas?"

"Ideas? Any ideas about what?" he said teasingly.

His voice sounded stronger. I was curious about what he looked like, after all these weeks out of hell, not being wounded and tortured, getting decent nourishment, being able to groom himself. I hadn't seen him since the day we had gone to Lola's, one day after he'd come back to earth. Not that I wanted to see him. I was just morbidly curious.

"Ideas about. . . ." I couldn't bring myself to actually say it. "Ideas about how to keep Rusty away from Jen. And how to stop him from killing Lola."

"Lola's irritating, of course," he said. "But she never did anything to deserve the life he's been inflicting on her all these years. And I wouldn't put it past him to do to you exactly what he's been threatening Jen he wants to do to you."

"What's he been threatening?" I didn't really want to know, but I couldn't keep from asking. "And how do you know, anyway?"

"Trang is my eyes and my ears, because Rusty doesn't know about him. Trang also cares about you, because of how he had to leave his wife. He feels for you. And he overheard Rusty telling Jen he wants to fix you so you can never be with a girl again."

For a moment I couldn't think of anything to say. Then I asked him, "I thought you said you were going to take care of him."

"You're child's play to him," Fleck said. "Lola's what counts, Lola's where the money is. He won't make his move against you until he's taken care of Lola first. Don't worry your little head."

If he didn't want me to worry, why was he telling me this?

"I've got to go," Fleck said. "But now you know Rusty. And you know the situation isn't going to get any better."

It didn't. One weekday evening when Mom was at work, there was a knock at the door. My heart thudded. Who could it be? Nobody ever came over here. Was it Fleck? Trang? "Who's there?" I called out.

There was no answer, just another knock.

I didn't know what to do.

And then the door slowly began to open. And I realized that I'd forgotten to lock it. How could I be so stupid? I ran to push it shut. But it was already a foot open and the person pushing it was stronger than I was. In seconds, Rusty stood inside the trailer.

He was all smiles, in his expensive clothes and watch, the lock of red hair falling so handsomely over his forehead. "Hey, Nick, how're you doing?" he said pleasantly, holding out his hand.

I didn't hold out mine. "What . . . what are you doing here?" I said, feeling terrified, and hating myself for it.

"Just wanted to pay you a little social call, see this great place you live in, admire your lovely thick hair. A lot of girls must be envious of your hair."

When he said that, my anger began creeping up, getting stronger than my fear. "How did you find out where I live?" I asked him.

"Are you stupid? I got your name from Jen, of course. Once you know the name, the address is so easy to find. Oh. Speaking of finding things. Did Jen tell you I found this?" He took the Swiss Army knife out of his pocket and flipped out one of the long blades. Opening Swiss knives can be hard. He was so good at it he could do it with one hand.

For some reason that only made me angrier. I felt like asking him if that was what he was going to use on Lola, but I wasn't that stupid. If he knew I knew he was planning to kill her, I'd be in a whole lot more danger than I was already. "I'm impressed," I said.

He snapped the knife shut again and put it back in his pocket. "I just wanted to let you know. Jen is wonderful. But you know that already. She's a prize, the most gorgeous girl I've ever known. I can't understand why she's been holding out for so long, not going all the way." He looked genuinely puzzled. "But she won't be able to resist much longer." He turned around, studying the trailer, keeping the puzzled expression. "She ever been here?"

"No," I said, but I didn't tell him the reason was that I was embarrassed for her to see it.

"I'll get her over to my house. That'll do the trick. My car, Longfellow House—and when she sees my house, and understands my prospects, she won't be able to resist." He looked me over. "I can see my body's a lot better than yours, too. I've been working out with weights for years. You're skinny."

I didn't have time to work out with weights, of course. "I'm skinny like a runner," I said, defending myself. "I ride my bike all the time. That's aerobic. Healthier than building up a lot of useless muscles."

"Useless? You should see how girls react when they

get a look at my body. That's worth every minute of pumping iron. So, I just wanted to say—leave Jen alone. Forget about her. Let her go. It's inevitable anyway. And you'll be better off if *you* do."

I knew what he meant by that, because of what Fleck had told me. But it wasn't an overt threat. Rusty wasn't stupid enough to make an overt threat. "You don't care what Jen wants, do you?" I asked him. "You just care about what you want."

He put his hand over his mouth and giggled. "You think she wants *this?*" he said, gesturing around at the trailer. "Or *this?*" he added, pushing his big strong hand against my chest. "Anyway, gotta go now. Just wanted to see where my *rival* lives," and he giggled again as he smoothly stepped out the door.

I called Fleck. "He just came to my house and threatened me," I said.

"I think it's time for me to show you something," Fleck said. "I'll be over right away."

I waited outside; I didn't want Fleck coming into the trailer and stinking it up again. Trang's car arrived in half an hour. When the door opened and the light came on, I saw a stranger in the driver's seat. I hesitated. He wore old unmatching clothes, Trang's clothes, too small for him, but they didn't hide the fact that he was handsome, with glossy black hair and chiseled features. It was only his green, green eyes that I recognized.

He must have noticed the surprise on my face. "Yes. Meet the real Fleck," he said smoothly, and I knew the voice immediately.

He had an old, cheap fake leather man's handbag on the seat beside him. "Come on in," he said, when I still hesitated. "Do you know someplace we can go around here where nobody will see or hear us?"

"What . . . what for?" I said, though I was beginning to get an idea—an idea I didn't like at all.

"You need a little lesson—in case something happens to me and you need to defend yourself against Rusty. They could whisk me back to hell at any minute, you know."

I was staring uneasily at the fake leather satchel. "I thought you said Lola was the main target—that he would take care of her first."

"I realized I was wrong about that after he threatened you. With a psycho like Rusty, you can never be sure," he said. He picked up the satchel and patted the seat. "Come on, come on, we haven't got all night. Don't want Mommy to wonder where you are."

I slid in and took the satchel uncomfortably. "You said you work in a hospital," Fleck said smoothly. "You better get us some of those surgical gloves, like by tomorrow. Don't want fingerprints on the gun, do we."

The trailer park was at the edge of town. Twenty minutes away was a huge plot of empty land that was slated to be developed as a subdivision. But they hadn't started building anything yet, so there were no guards and no people. There were also no lights, and we didn't want to leave the car lights on just in case that might attract some attention. So I had to learn how to use the gun in the darkness, with only the moon and stars.

It was remarkably easy to understand the mechanism. Of course they make guns easy to work on purpose—the gun makers and gun sellers don't want only smart people buying killing weapons. They want to make money from everybody, even people with low IQs, and especially people who are too stupid to think before acting.

After he had explained to me how to do it, Fleck told me to stand in front of him, facing away from him. "When you shoot, be prepared for the recoil. It'll push back hard," he told me.

He was right. The first time I shot, I pointed it

slightly toward the ground, so all it would hit was earth. The recoil was much stronger than I expected—they don't show that in the movies. My arm was pushed all the way back against my chest, and the shot went haywire. I dared to shoot it one more time, and this time before I pulled the trigger I held my arm as taut as possible. My muscles might not be as bulky as Rusty's, but I rode my bike everywhere and I was wiry and strong, more than he knew. This time my arm hardly bounced back at all, and the shot went smoothly. "Now let's get out of here," I said, and we did.

"You know I'm never going to use that thing," I told Fleck, pushing the satchel away when he dropped me off.

"Of course I know you won't, pal," he said, smiling in his genial way. "This lesson was just for your own protection, in case something happens to me. Oh, and tomorrow's Friday. I'm tired of letting Trang have all the fun. How about you and me following Jen and Rusty tomorrow night and seeing what they're up to. I bet you're curious."

"I don't think that's a good idea," I said.

"But you are curious, aren't you?" he goaded me. "Anyway, do you really think she's safe with a psycho like him? Don't you think we ought to look out for her? I'm doing you a favor, you know—you couldn't go fast enough on your bike to keep up with his Fiat."

"Pick me up here after I get back from work," I said.

13

Fleck was waiting for me at the trailer when I got home from work the next evening. I locked up my bike and opened the door of Trang's car. The fake leather handbag with the gun in it was on the passenger seat. "Come on, hurry it up," Fleck said. "He already picked her up. I was staking out her house."

I didn't like that. "What if he'd seen you?" I asked him, as I got in and reluctantly pulled the satchel onto my lap. "He might still recognize you after eight years. And why did you have to bring the gun?"

He grinned. "He was only ten when he killed me. Anyway, he wouldn't pay any attention to a car like this or whoever might be in it. It's beneath his notice. And as for the gun . . . well, what if we have to protect Jen? Where are the gloves?"

"Gloves?" I said, confused.

"I told you to bring gloves from the hospital, so there won't be any fingerprints."

"Oh. I forgot."

"Remember them tomorrow. I just hope nothing happens tonight," he said grimly, and revved the engine and drove off, almost as fast as Trang.

I had gotten in trouble for being late for work, because of teachers calling me in after school for conferences about the decline in my schoolwork. Now Rusty was interfering with my chances for getting into college. But I didn't feel like talking about that with Fleck. I put on the safety belt, which was hard to adjust because it was ragged. I slumped silently down in the seat, feeling the weight of the gun in my lap. I didn't like spying on Rusty and Jen with Fleck. I was only going along with this because I really was worried about Jen.

Fleck drove fast, but he was much smoother and more careful than Trang, and he didn't smoke. He went right downtown, and found the red Fiat parked in front of a fancy hotel.

I didn't feel like talking to Fleck, but at the sight of that I couldn't control myself. "He took her to a *hotel?*" I shouted.

"I followed them here," he said. "Rusty got the last parking place on the street, and they went inside. Then I had to go back to pick you up because you work so damned late. It gets in the way. Maybe you should think about—"

"Don't tell me to quit my job," I said to him. "They'll probably fire me before I get a chance to quit, anyway."

"You're really letting Rusty screw over your whole life, aren't you," he said.

"Shut up! Did you see if they checked in, or what? I can't believe this. Rusty told me last night that Jen wouldn't put out for him."

"Maybe they're just eating," Fleck said. "I better check it out myself. They'd recognize you much faster than me. You wait here."

He was double parked on a busy street. "But what if a cop comes along?" I said. "Here I am with a *gun.*"

"Drive around the block if anybody gives you trouble," he said, getting out of the car. "I'll meet you here." He slammed the door and strode into the hotel.

How was he going to find out if they had checked in or not? I hated this. I almost preferred not to know what they were doing. Except that I really was worried about Jen. Rusty was so crazy.

Two minutes after Fleck got out of the car a cop came along on a motorcycle and rapped on the driver's side window. I had no choice but to slide over and roll it down. I prayed he wouldn't notice the old satchel I left on the passenger seat, which had the gun in it.

The cop frowned when he got a look at my hair. He gestured with his gloved hand. "Move along, move along," he said. "No stopping here."

I had gotten my driver's license when I was sixteen. They had driver training at school, where they showed you movies of horrible accidents and people screaming things like, "Oh, my leg! My leg!" They taught you how to drive an automatic car, like my Mom's, which I had taken the test in. This one had a stick shift. I had no idea how to use it.

The cop was waiting for me to move the car. I looked at the gear shift and the extra pedal on the floor. I forced myself not to look at the handbag with the gun in it. Did I dare to tell the cop I didn't know how to drive this thing? Why had Fleck put me in this horrible situation?

And then Fleck showed up. "Excuse me, officer,"

he said to the cop, standing tall and straight and businesslike, looking good even in Trang's old clothes. "We'll be going now. Sorry to cause you any problem." He nodded pleasantly at the cop, whose expression changed. The cop nodded back at him. Fleck sure knew how to win people over.

I slid back into the passenger seat. Fleck got in and drove away. He turned right at the first corner and the cop peeled away down the main street.

"What if he'd caught me with the gun?" I said angrily. "And I don't know how to drive this thing."

Fleck didn't pay any attention. "You'll be relieved to know they were in the restaurant," he told me. "Rusty was giving the waiter a hard time about the food not being cooked right." Mom complained about customers like that, who blamed the waitperson for everything, and then didn't tip them. "We'll just have to drive around until they leave. Needless to say, neither of us has the money to park in a lot."

So we drove aimlessly around in the traffic. I worried about the gun. I was fuming about Fleck dragging me along on this pointless and unpleasant excursion, but I was fuming a lot more about Rusty. And worried about where he would take Jen after this.

Fleck had exceptional luck, and just happened to

pass the hotel for the tenth time when Rusty was pulling his red Fiat out of the parking place. He managed to follow Rusty through the traffic. And then there was less traffic, and the convertible's automatic roof went up, and they were heading for Highland Drive.

My heart sank. "Do we have to watch this?" I asked.

"What if she fights him off and he threatens her?" Fleck said helpfully.

We couldn't see much. The street lights were few and far between here, which was the whole point, and Rusty's lights were off and we had to turn ours off too. We stopped about twenty feet behind them, with no other cars in between.

And then we just waited. We couldn't see inside Rusty's car. But as far as I could tell, no struggle seemed to be going on. It was horrible being here, and imagining what they were doing in the car. I literally felt sick. I kept looking at my watch, and after ten minutes I said, "How long do we have to stay here?"

"Long enough to be sure Jen is safe," Fleck said.

"But how can we even tell? And what are we going to do if she isn't safe?" I asked him.

He patted the gun.

"Not me," I said. "No way."

I could see him lifting his hands in the darkness. "I never said you had to touch it," he said innocently. "Not unless something happens to me, and you or Jen is in danger. I'm just helping you. Why do you resent it so much?"

There was no answer to that question. Time dragged on endlessly. At ten-fifteen they finally left, and Jen went into her house at ten-thirty. As much as her mother probably loved Rusty, her curfew still seemed to be the same.

Finally Fleck dropped me off. "Call me when you get out of work tomorrow," he said.

I didn't even try to stifle my groan. "How long do we have to keep doing this?"

"How long do we have to make sure Jen is safe? And this time, don't forget the gloves."

I knew there was a soccer game the next day, Saturday. I remembered to take a box of nonlatex gloves from the hospital—they were all over the place there. We got to Jen's house in the late afternoon. We parked several houses away and across the street. Soon after that, Rusty and Jen drove up in the convertible. It was light enough for us to see clearly that they kissed each other before getting out of the car. I thought I could see that Jen didn't look very happy, but I was still burning inside. Why was Fleck inflicting this on me?

He seemed to be able to read my thoughts. "You're doing this for her," he said, smiling at me. I felt like strangling him.

Rusty was wearing an expensive lavender polo shirt that was tighter than usual, emphasizing his bulging biceps and pectorals and small waist. Did he think that would turn Jen on? *Did* it turn her on? Jen still had on her soccer uniform. They went into the house together. Jen would shower and change. Rusty would talk charmingly with her parents. I felt like I was going crazy.

Fleck was whistling in an irritating way. He knew he was torturing me, and he was enjoying every minute of it.

At least Fleck was still wearing Trang's old threadbare clothes, pants too short, always clashing with the garish shirts. The only satisfaction I had was knowing that he still didn't have any money. I wondered vaguely how he was paying for the gas to follow Rusty and Jen around.

After forty-five endless minutes Rusty and Jen came out of the house. Jen was wearing an expensive-looking dress that I had never seen before, which was held up by spaghetti straps over the shoulders. I was surprised her parents were letting her wear something that sexy. I couldn't help wondering if Rusty had bought it for her. I had never been able to afford to give her anything like that.

Rusty seemed more animated than usual, talking and laughing. Jen kept smiling at him. They were too far away for me to read her expression carefully, but it did seem to me that her smile was artificial. But I was probably only imagining that because it was what I wanted to believe.

Fleck kept whistling as he started the car to follow them. I wanted to scream at him to shut up, but I felt too morose to say anything.

And then, as we followed them into a fancier neighborhood, Fleck's whistling gradually stopped. Finally he murmured, "I don't believe this."

"What don't you believe? What do you mean?"

"It looks like . . . like he's heading for his house. He didn't seem to have much trouble convincing her to go with him."

"Thanks for pointing that out," I said.

"Bingo!" Fleck said, a few blocks later, when we saw them going through a security check point. "That's his neighborhood, all right. Gated and secured, of course." We watched one of the guards salute Rusty and wave him through.

"So we can't follow them," I said, almost feeling relieved.

"Wrong," Fleck said. "I know the secret back way, of course. We won't be able to drive right to the house, but we couldn't do that anyway because someone would notice. But I know how to get close enough so that we can walk."

"But *why?*" I asked him, feeling worse than ever. "What can we possibly *do* there?"

"Do you think he cares if she meets his parents?" Fleck asked me, backing up the car and turning onto a side street. "I'll bet you a million bucks his parents are out of town. I know they travel all the time. Why else would he want to bring her to his house? This is the whole reason we're following them."

I shook my head wearily, the bag with the gun sitting on my lap. "Can't we just leave them alone? Can't you just take me home?"

"You can imagine what Rusty gets like when he doesn't get his own way," Fleck said. "And the grounds are very large—the other houses in the neighborhood are too far away for anybody to hear."

"To hear what?" I wanted to know.

"Do you think Rusty's father doesn't have his own gun collection?" Fleck asked me. "He has them hidden all over the house, too, in case of somebody trying to break in."

"Are you telling me he's going to shoot her if she resists him?" I asked him. "He can't be *that* crazy!"

"Yes he can," Fleck said with certainty. "Don't forget, he killed me. And he's going to kill Lola any day now. That's the other reason we have to keep our eyes on him."

"I don't get it," I said. "He's already so loaded. Why does he have to kill you and Lola to get even *more* money?"

"It's called greed," Fleck said dryly. "He wants it all. We know that because of what he did to me. The medical term is—"

"Psychopath," I interrupted him. "I know that already. Man, do I know it. But he's not going to kill Jen. Then he'd never get her to do what he wants."

"Sometimes he loses control," Fleck said, and parked the car next to a locked gate in a metal fence.

The little back entrance was obscure; you would never know it led to a rich neighborhood. The fence wasn't very high—whoever put it there wasn't very worried about security from this point.

"Come on, buddy," Fleck said. "We can climb over the fence. Don't forget the gun. Give me a pair of gloves and put some on yourself."

I hesitated. I didn't want to break in like this.

"That maniac is alone with Jen," Fleck reminded me. "He could do anything."

I thought of Rusty's pathologically self-involved Web site. "Okay, okay," I said.

Climbing over the fence wasn't hard for me, even carrying the gun. Fleck had more trouble than I did. That gave me a certain amount of bitter satisfaction.

Inside it was all lawns and big shade trees. I had never been anywhere like it. Fleck pointed at a huge white house with a columned portico and a swimming pool in the back. The Fiat was parked in the semicircular driveway. It was the only car there. "Just like I said, his parents aren't here," Fleck said. "And I bet he's not wasting any time, either."

There were no other houses nearby, but I could see that Fleck was trying to keep hidden behind trees and shrubbery, so I followed his example. "But what are we going to do?" I asked him.

"Rusty won't be expecting that anybody followed them. You're the only one who'd want to, and he knows all you have is that bike, which can't go fast enough. We can peek inside, see what's going on, make sure Jen is safe."

"But what do you think he's going to *do?*" I wanted to know. "If he hurt her, other people could see something had happened to her. She'd tell her parents. They—"

"Rusty can buy his way out of anything. Remember what he threatened to do to you? And he seems to be being patient with Jen. That's not natural for him. At any minute he's going to crack—unless he gets his way."

I just wanted to get out of here. I hated spying on them. But what if Fleck was right, as he was about so many things, and something *did* happen to Jen? Something I could have prevented? I would never forgive myself.

There was a hedge around the driveway, so we could get up close to the house while staying hidden. Rusty wouldn't be watching out for us anyway. And it was beginning to get dark. Fleck led me toward a big window. "This is the living room," he whispered. "We can start here."

There was only one light on; most of the room was in shadow. But you could still see that it was a beautiful room, all potted plants and Oriental rugs, and paintings on the walls. There were two big overstuffed white couches, facing each other.

The light was over one of the couches, where Rusty was lying on top of Jen, and she was struggling.

"That . . . that *asshole!*" I said in a whisper so harsh it surprised me.

Rusty was stronger than she was. He was pulling the lovely new dress down off her shoulders by the spaghetti straps. The house was well insulated, and there was probably central air conditioning. But we could still hear her screaming at him to stop. Pointlessly screaming. Because no one else could hear, and he wasn't stopping, and the dress was coming down off her shoulders.

I was so furious I felt like smashing the window and running inside.

"Rape," Fleck said, in what could only be called a growl. "He's got to be threatened or he won't stop. Give me the gun."

We were both wearing the surgical gloves. He pulled the gun out of the satchel and headed for the front door.

"But how are we going to get in?" I asked him. I was boiling with rage and had no hesitation about getting in there and stopping Rusty. The two of us, with Jen, could probably do it.

"Trang got Lola's key; she has it from the days when she was still part of the family social life. And I remember the security code. But we still have to be as quiet as possible so he won't hear anything and try to shoot us. I told you, this house always has a gun hidden safely nearby in case anybody ever tries to break in."

At the door, Fleck took a key from his pocket and inserted it into the lock. He turned it carefully; it clicked softly. He began to pull it open very slowly. The door was in good repair, well-oiled, and made no sound.

As it opened, the sounds from inside got louder.

"Relax, bitch!" Rusty was shouting, his voice trembling and out of breath.

"Stop it!" Jen screamed, and I could hear the tears in her voice.

I wanted to roar and pummel Rusty.

Fleck ran inside into an entrance hallway and I followed. He quickly pushed the keys on the security system, then shouted, "Stop it!" and even in the middle of all this I wondered why he wasn't being quiet, as he had just told me we had to be. It was almost as though he was warning Rusty that we were coming.

Their voices were to the left of us. We ran through a wide arched opening.

Rusty was pushing himself up off Jen. She was struggling to get out from under him, and pulling up the straps of her dress.

As soon as Rusty saw Fleck he jumped to his feet. He was so shocked to see Fleck alive that he didn't seem afraid of the gun Fleck was waving at him. And in a moment he had jumped Fleck and pinned him to the Oriental rug. The gun flew out of Fleck's hand, and off the rug, and slid over the wooden floor, out of Rusty's reach. Rusty was sitting on top of Fleck and punching him mercilessly.

"Nick!" Jen cried, her voice flooded with relief. "How did you . . ."

Fleck struggled, but he was no match for Rusty. Rusty was pummeling him so hard that in a minute his nose would be broken, or an eye would be put out. And even as he was doing this, I could see that Rusty was squirming to get close to a small table with a drawer in it.

A gun was probably hidden there, as Fleck had said.

Jen ran toward me, but I had to stop Rusty first. I dropped the old leather satchel and ran over and picked up Fleck's gun from the floor.

"Stop it!" I shouted at Rusty. "Stop it or I'll shoot!"

Rusty ignored me completely. He gave Fleck a really hard punch to the chin, which seemed to daze him, and then reached over to open the drawer.

Without thinking, I held the gun out in my arms, stiff and straight, took careful aim, and pulled the trigger.

The sound was deafening in there. And when the bullet hit Rusty in the forehead, it wasn't like in the movies, with one neat little round hole. Blood and brains splashed pink mush all over the Oriental rug as he toppled over, falling off of Fleck, his head smashing into a glass coffee table.

Jen screamed. She didn't stop screaming. I had to make her quiet. But I had to be careful, too. I picked up the satchel and put the gun inside it. Then I ran over to her—*not* looking at what was sprawled over the coffee table—and put my arm around her and pulled her to me.

She stopped screaming and started crying and crying. "How could you? Oh, my God! How could you? *How could you?*"

"I had to! I had to save you from him, Jen. I didn't mean it to be like this. But he's killed before, and he was going to again, and you would never be safe with him. For more reasons than you know. Now we've got to get out of here."

I turned back to Fleck. He was slowly climbing to his feet. It was so dark now, with only one little lamp behind him, that I couldn't see what Rusty had done to his face.

"Are you okay? Can you walk? Can you drive?" I asked him.

Even now, Fleck made a guttural laugh. "Sure I can, pal," he said, his voice rough. "This wasn't much of anything compared to what I've been through."

Jen was still crying, her hand over her eyes, not really looking at Fleck. "Who's he?" she whimpered.

"Somebody who wanted to help you, who was afraid for you, because he knows Rusty better than anybody."

"We better . . . get out of here," Fleck said.

I started maneuvering Jen toward the front door. She was in such a state of shock that she could barely walk. I had to support her and guide her with one arm. I couldn't just leave the satchel here because it probably had my fingerprints from before all over it. The gun probably did, too, even though this time I had been wearing gloves. I would have to throw it away somewhere obscure.

Fleck opened the door, and we went out into the night and around the house. Jen was still leaning limply against me and crying.

"Jen, Jen, he was reaching for a gun. And he was going to kill somebody—somebody who's been hiding from him for eight years. That's how he was going to get all the money he kept bragging about. He already killed one person who was in his way. He could have killed you any time. I was so worried. Jen, you know he was crazy. I had to do it. Jen, we've got to get out of here."

"But . . . how *could* you?" she kept whimpering.

"It was a mistake, an accident."

"He would have shot us if Nick hadn't done it," Fleck said. "He had a gun in that drawer."

I pulled her toward the metal fence, trying to get her to move faster. At least she was quiet now. I looked quickly around. There didn't seem to be any reactions from any of the other houses.

And then an alarm began to sound from Rusty's house, like a siren. I knew those things were connected to a police station. The cops would be here right away.

"Damn!" Fleck muttered. "You have to reset the alarm when you go out of the house. I clean forgot."

At least nobody was coming out of any of the other houses; they probably thought it was a malfunction. Fleck and I both pushed and pulled Jen over the fence. Athletic as she was, she was in such a state of shock that both of us had to help her get over it to the car. She slumped limply in the back seat. I sat in front with Fleck, the satchel still in my gloved hands.

Fleck drove fast, away from the fence, through the little tangle of small streets, out onto the main street. Finally we were safe here—safe from everybody except Jen herself.

But now she wasn't limp and whimpering. She was sitting up straighter, getting more normal. "Listen, Jen. What I told you is true. He already killed one guy, and he was planning to kill this woman, so he'd have even *more* money. And I found out what he said he was going to do to me. He could have hurt you bad, Jen. He *was* hurting you! We just came here to protect you from him. I didn't mean to do it like that. It just happened."

She gulped. But she wasn't hysterical anymore. "But what's going to happen to *you?*" she said in a breathy voice.

"Nothing's going to happen to him," Fleck said. "Rusty was going to shoot us. It was self-defense."

Jen didn't say anything. She had asked about Fleck once, but now it was as though he didn't exist to her.

Suddenly I realized I was more scared of her than anything else. Did I dare leave her with her parents? Could she ever love me after this? I now had a deep conviction that she couldn't. A cold, cold feeling ran through me. I had saved Jen and Lola—and lost Jen.

"Jen, please, please, don't say anything. You know me. I did it for *good*, to protect you, and other people! Fleck's right, it was self-defense. Do you think the world is going to be a worse place without that murdering, greedy psycho? Did you know he came to my house and threatened me with a knife? He was reaching for a gun. What else could I do? Please, please, don't say anything."

"Sure, Nick," she said, in an almost normal voice. Scarily normal.

"Jen, you saw what happened. It was the only way to protect you. Promise me you won't tell your parents. Promise me. Please, Jen."

"Like I said, it was self-defense," Fleck tried to remind her.

"Why would I tell my parents?" she said, continuing to ignore Fleck. "It would just make everything worse."

"Right, right, you got it. Now you understand. Tell them what happened, that he made a violent physical attack on you, it's the truth! And you fought him off and then made him drive you home. Then just go to bed. I'll see you tomorrow. Promise me. Please promise me!"

"Of course I'll promise you," she said. "I just . . . never saw anybody get his head blown off before. It made me . . . lose control for awhile." She sighed deeply. "But . . . I'm okay now. I promise. You can trust me."

But could I? I told her, over and over again, to tell them what he had really done to her. It was the truth. And she kept sounding more and more normal. Still, when we dropped her off at her house I felt more tense than I ever had in my life.

I worried all the way home. But I still didn't want to talk to Fleck about her. "Too bad the alarm went off," I said.

He hit his forehead with his fist. "How could I be so stupid?" he said.

"And what about this?" I said, lifting the satchel with the gun in it.

"I'll take care of that," he said. "You don't need to worry about it at all," he assured me.

When we got back to the trailer, he reached out to shake my hand before I got out of the car. "Congratulations, pal. We just saved three people—Jen, Lola, and probably you, too. We did a good deed. That's all it was."

I got out of the car and hurried inside.

And then I paced, worrying, clutching the cell phone. It still hadn't sunk in that I had really killed somebody. I was worried about what Jen was going to do. I had never seen her behave the way she had after I had killed him.

Forty-five minutes later there was a knock at the door. Who could it be? Fleck coming to congratulate me again? It had to be him. No one else but Jen knew anything about it. And Jen wouldn't come here now. I slipped the cell phone in my pocket to be sure it was safe, and opened the door.

Four cops stood there. The one in front was holding a pair of handcuffs. Two others were pointing guns at me and the fourth was pointing a flashlight. I felt like I'd been hit by a powerful electric shock. "What . . . what *is* this?" I said.

"We're arresting you for the murder of Rusty Girard. We'll read you your rights in the car." Before I knew it the front cop had snapped the handcuffs around my wrists. And then he was pulling me—none too gently—toward the waiting police car with the red light flashing.

"Hey, look at this." The cop with the flashlight bent over and picked up the old fake leather satchel. He poked the satchel with one hand. "There's a gun in here. And right here in the driveway."

Right here in the driveway—where Fleck had left it.

Mom wept quietly throughout the trial. That was bad enough.

Worst of all was the fact that it had been Jen who turned me in. She had still been in shock, putting on an act, when we left her outside her parents' house that night. Inside, she broke down and told them Rusty had attacked her and I had shot him. She was vague about Fleck; she had never gotten a good look at him in the darkness, and was too distraught to pay attention to what a stranger said. They had called the cops immediately. And here I was, on trial for murder—with the murder weapon conveniently outside my house, and an eyewitness who had formerly been my girlfriend.

Lola was there, too, looking very different. She wasn't scared and weepy anymore. She was calm. She had on a fancy black dress, and pearls, and an elaborately styled hairdo, and she was perfectly made up. She was beautiful.

A man was with her. Once again, I didn't recognize him right away—it had been a long time between the arrest and the trial. He was tall and good-looking, with thick black hair, wearing an expensive suit with a jeweled tie clip. It was his green, green eyes that gave him away this time too. Fleck, even more recovered after all this time, and with an altered face. He'd had plastic surgery, made his nose smaller, his cheekbones higher. He was wearing beautiful clothes like Lola was. Fleck and Lola sitting next to each other, whispering like best friends.

And they *were* friends, of course. They had always been friendly cousins. And together they tricked me into getting them Rusty's fortune. Lola had only been pretending to be afraid of Fleck. She must have known he was around the whole time. It seemed ridiculous now that I had ever believed his story about hell. Their plan was crazy, but clever, and I had fallen for it.

Fleck was jaunty, his eyes bright, meeting my gaze directly. Lola, at least, seemed uncomfortable when I was on the stand, avoiding looking at me. In her expensive clothes she was pretending to be mourning for Rusty.

Trang came, too, looking very, very sad. He had tried, he had returned the phone, he had warned me not to listen to them, not to trust either of them. And I had stupidly ignored him. Why hadn't he done more? He was too passive, under their control. When he was with them, he did what they said.

Of course I could not afford a good defense lawyer. My lawyer was a hack provided by the state. There wasn't much in it for him even if I was acquitted. And anyway, he believed I was guilty.

Rusty's parents—his mother in a black veil, his father in a black suit—sat in the front row. They were powerful people and had put a lot of pressure on the prosector's office to try me as an adult.

At least Trang testified in my favor. Both of us told the whole story, about the phone, about how Lola and Fleck would inherit a fortune if Rusty died, about how they had set me up to do it. They had known what would happen when Rusty met Jen, how he would be compelled to do everything he could to get her away from me. That was his way, he was competitive about everything. But did that matter? I had still killed him, and *not* in self-defense. I had shot him cold-bloodedly in the head. And he hadn't had a gun in his hand.

And the prosecution had evidence that Fleck had died eight years ago. Faked, I guess. Anyway Jen hadn't seen him well enough to be able to identify him. And, he looked different now than he had that night. It was clear that the court believed that everything Trang and I said about Fleck was a lie, or a delusion.

My lawyer made a pathetic attempt to get me off on an insanity plea, but they had given me tests, and I was clearly not insane. I was just a jealous, murderous fool. It didn't help that there had been a shooting at a nearby high school the year before. Violence in schools—and therefore among teenagers—was a major fear in our community. That didn't make the jury feel anymore compassionate toward me. The prosecution's story was that I had done it in a jealous rage. They emphasized that it wasn't just Jen I was jealous of, but the fact that Rusty was so much richer than I was. I had nothing and he had everything. Jen was at least truthful enough to testify how aggressive Rusty was, and how threatening. But Rusty hadn't done anything lethal, and I had.

All my studying and working and riding my bike

everywhere and doing my grade-A homework by hand did nothing in my defense.

The jury deliberated for only one hour. The verdict of first degree murder was unanimous. And then came the sentencing.

"Due to the gravity of the crime," said the judge, "and the fact that it was clearly premeditated—and because now there is a national epidemic of lethal crimes among teenagers—we have decided to sentence this seventeen-year-old as an adult." He banged his gavel. "We must do everything in our power to show these violent teenagers that they can *no longer* get away with crimes like this. This is not an unprecedented decision. And so the sentence is death by lethal injection."

There was an uproar in the court. Mom was bent over, openly sobbing now. Rusty's parents were hugging each other. Jen went completely pale. And as they led me out I could hear her screaming at me, "Nick! Nick! I didn't know they would do this. If I'd known, I never, never would have—"

They pulled me out of the courtroom.

Since I had been tried as an adult, they didn't put me in a juvenile detention center to wait for the execution day. They put me in with other convicted murderers in my own cell, because of how dangerous the other inmates here were.

I was going crazy, of course, alternating between rage and despair. Fleck and Lola were the real criminals. I had been their dumb dupe. I banged my fist against the iron bed over and over again, until it bled. How could I have been so stupid? It all seemed so obvious to me now. They could have been staking me out for months in advance, I was such a perfect fool for them and their bizarre charade. Poor, so that I'd be envious of everything Rusty had. With a beautiful girlfriend who was exactly the kind of girl Rusty would go for and aggressively take away from me. I was precisely what they needed to get their fortune for them.

The guy at the discount store could have been part of it, too. It would have been easy for them to bribe him to send me the flier about cheap phones and then sell me Trang's phone, with the number they knew and no caller ID. With my hair, I would be easy for him to recognize. Probably one of many plans they'd had had for making contact with me. Or maybe they'd just figured that *anyone* who bought the phone would be desperate enough to help. Anyway their plan had worked.

People were occasionally allowed to come and visit me and talk to me via microphone through a thick plastic panel. Mom took time off work to come during visiting hours. She cried whenever she came; I dreaded her visits. "You were always such a good boy, Nick. Working so hard, doing so well in school. What went wrong? How did you change so much? Was it my fault for being away from you so much of the time?"

I assured her over and over again that it wasn't her fault at all. I just kept insisting on what had really happened, how Fleck and Lola had cleverly put me into a position where it was almost inevitable that I would kill Rusty, so they'd get the money. That didn't make any difference to her. She didn't believe me. She always left even more miserable because I wouldn't change my story.

Jen came once. I knew her parents were waiting just outside the room—they didn't want her coming here. She cried, too. "I had no idea this would happen," she kept saying. "Oh, God, Nick, I miss you. I'll never stop missing you. Do you blame me? Is it all my fault?"

If only we could have held hands. I still loved her, but my feelings were very mixed now. She had deserted me for Rusty. And, even worse, she had told her parents instead of protecting me. I knew she had been out of control, that the incident had shocked her beyond belief. So I loved her, but now there was resentment in my feelings for her that had never been there before. "If you had known I would get death, would you have *not* told them?" I asked her.

She looked at me pleadingly, her face tear-stained. "Oh, Nick, I don't know, I don't know. It was just so horrifying. It was unreal, a nightmare, you shooting him in the head." She wept into her hands. The guard came and took her away, and she kept looking back at me and crying and saying, "I miss you, Nick." That was the last time I saw her.

They let me have books in my cell, but I couldn't concentrate. My emotions veered from fury to grief. I didn't feel guilty—the world *was* better without Rusty. But why did it have to be me who had to die for it? I felt stupid, stupid, stupid. I had been a gullible fool to fall for their game.

I also couldn't help wondering about one huge thing: Did hell really exist? And if it did, was Fleck right that you didn't go there if the crime you committed was to save somebody, or if you believed you were saving somebody?

The question was, *had* I killed Rusty just to help Jen? Partly, yes. But another part of it *was* jealousy and envy. Did that mean I *would* go to hell?

This was something I tried not to think about. But I couldn't concentrate on books, I couldn't stop blaming myself and hating Fleck and Lola. And I couldn't stop thinking about hell.

When Mom visited and she wasn't crying, she told me there were protests about giving me the death penalty because I was so young. I knew that already; they did let you watch TV in here. But the governor was adamant. I was an example. My death would stop other teenaged murderers.

The food was terrible, and I hardly ate anything. They made us walk around in the prison yard every day, but that wasn't like real exercise. I was skinnier than I had ever been. There were hardly any mirrors, but when I did happen to pass one, I didn't look in it. I stopped shaving and brushing my teeth. What difference did it make?

I felt dread, but I was also impatient. I thought about what Fleck had said about hell. What he had described was too crazy—the drunken karaoke, the corruption, subjecting yourself to extra torture in order to earn rewards such as phoning the earth. It was a fairy tale. He had made it all up. If he hadn't looked and smelled so hideous—and the phone hadn't acted so crazy—I wouldn't have believed a word.

I would die and then there would be nothing. It was scary, but it would be better than this.

Then I was told that no doctor would be there for my execution—doctors could not be involved because of medical ethics. It would be done by an orderly. And what orderly could be very experienced at doing this, since there were no other executions happening in this prison?

That was when I really began to get scared.

The execution chamber was small. I didn't struggle, but they still shackled my feet and my left hand to the hospital-type bed. In my right hand I held the cursed cell phone against my chest. My last request was to have it with me. Everyone thought this was crazy, but the warden had permitted it. I didn't know why I wanted the phone; it had been the cause of all this—the cell phone and my own stupidity. It was a gut feeling that I wanted it with me now.

The minister had already come to my cell and talked to me about God. I didn't listen. I knew the minister meant well, but I was still hardly even polite to him. I was depressed and I was bitter. But mostly I was mad at myself. I'd had a chance for a good life—not easy, but possible. And because I was stupid enough to fall for Fleck and Lola's plan, it was all over now.

The minister had also told me something about the execution. First they injected Sodium Pentothal to make me sleep. Next something called pancuronium bromide. Last came the potassium chloride. The minister was vague about what that drug would do to me.

Now here I was, strapped to the gurney in the execution chamber, terrified of what was going to happen next.

The orderly doing this was young, he seemed to be only a few years older than I was. He was unshaven and did not wear hospital gloves. Why bother? How could an infection hurt me now? He was appropriately somber, but still talkative. And why not? He was the only one in the chamber with me, now that I was strapped down.

"Just gotta get this IV in, first thing," he said. He took the hand that was strapped down and swiveled it not too gently so the palm faced up. He reached behind him and grabbed a syringe from a small table.

It was attached to a tube that went through a hole in the wall. There was no sign in the chamber of an IV tower or any bags of medication. It seemed the procedure would be done from outside the chamber—where my reactions to the various drugs could not be closely or directly observed or monitored.

Once he got the IV in, that is.

The orderly jabbed the needle into my wrist. "Damn!" he said. "Missed the vein." The stinging needle pierced my skin and a drop of blood appeared. Instinctively I tried to writhe away, but I couldn't move. The orderly clucked his teeth and shook his head. "Always happens to me," he complained, preparing to stick me in another place.

Always happens to *him?* What about what was happening to me?

Again he tried and failed to get the needle in the right place. It hurt more this time. The more he tried, the harder it was going to get. What if he ran out of places?

He kept puncturing my wrist, and missing, and swearing to himself. The wrist was now covered with bloody holes. Each time he tried to hit the vein, it hurt more and more. How could they get someone so inept to do this?

Half a painful hour later the IV was in. He taped it to my wrist, messily, over all the smeared blood already there. It hurt continuously, and I couldn't help moaning, and jerking away, and every time I did it hurt more.

"You'll feel better when we put in that Sodium Pento-whatever, man," he tried to reassure me. "And once that next drug goes in, I forget the name, you won't be able to move anyway, so it won't hurt." The needle in place, he turned and left the room without another word.

A minute or so later I felt something moving into my arm. The needle quivered, which increased the pain. And I felt nothing from the drug. I was now sweating and moaning even more. I had never been so scared in my life.

And then I began to feel drowsy. I didn't know whether to feel relief, or to be even more horrified. This was the last thing I would ever feel. The needle was still quivering. But now I didn't feel it so much, and my eyelids began to close.

In what seemed like only a few moments, my eyelids slowly opened. The knockout drug, Sodium Pentothal, didn't seem to last for very long. I tried to look down at my wrist with the IV in it.

I couldn't move my head, I couldn't move my free hand with the phone in it, I couldn't move at all. This was so much worse than I had imagined. A scream tried to come bursting out of me. All I did was choke. I couldn't make a sound.

This must be the pancuronium bromide. The orderly had said once they gave me the next drug I wouldn't be able to move. He hadn't said it would paralyze me. But that's what it was doing.

What was the point of paralyzing me when I was already strapped down with the IV in? And the paralysis gradually began to get worse. Breathing became more and more difficult. I instinctively gasped for breath, but I couldn't move. It was a continuous feeling of choking. It felt as though my air passage was shrinking, slowly shrinking. I lay there unable to move, and bit by tiny bit losing the ability to breathe. The pain of it was unimaginable. Why weren't they doing something about it? Why weren't they checking on me and stopping this agony?

I could see nobody through the small window in the chamber. Had they forgotten about me? I lay there for what seemed like hours, slowly being strangled. The words "Hanged by the neck until dead" came into my mind. This lethal injection was just as painful as that must have been.

Bathed in sweat, unable to scream, feeling the unbearable choking sensation, not drowsy at all, strangling . . . strangling . . .

The next thing I knew, I was standing in filth in a vast crowd. The smell was worse than a bathroom in a rundown bus station where the toilets don't flush. Filthy, emaciated people limped and staggered and crawled all around me, ignoring me, in a desperate hurry. I heard screams of pain not very far away.

And from everywhere came blasting the amplified sound of drunk people singing "Love Shack," out of tune, and laughing.

So Fleck *had* been here. And now *I* was the one who wanted out. Without thinking, I slipped the cell phone into the pocket of my orange prison pants. The phone and the attachments just barely fit, and part of the battery stuck out a little.

The needle and the bandage were gone, but blood was still dripping out of the numerous open punctures in my left wrist. If any of the wounds touched anything here, a horrible infection would result, everything was so filthy. Judging from the way people around me looked—and the way Fleck had looked when he first came back—infections *could* happen in hell. After all, germs and bugs and worms eat dead bodies; being dead wouldn't protect you from them. And it would go on forever.

The buildings were mostly cement, many with gaping holes in them spewing out smoke. They looked like they had been bombed in a war. A lot of them were surrounded by barbed wire. Old wrecked cars lay around rusting.

But far, far in the distance, on hilltops, you could catch glimpses of shining, unreachable palaces, surrounded by lush gardens. Their existence made everything else seem even worse.

Down here the filth on the ground was crusted with brown ice. I was hugging myself in the freezing cold.

"And just when things were starting to get good," a familiar voice said behind me, sounding out of breath. I spun around. I couldn't believe it.

Fleck was stooped over, looking furtively around, panting, his breath steaming in the cold. "Oh, *here*," he said, gasping. "The Square of Despair." He looked odd among all these bedraggled people with his shiny hair and smooth complexion, his fancy sports coat and open-necked shirt. His clothes wouldn't stay fancy for long, and his face wouldn't stay smooth. So it was *all* true. They had finally found him and taken him back. I felt a flicker of pleasure. He deserved to be here more than ever now.

Trang stood beside him, his mouth hanging open, holding his nose.

As much as I hated Fleck, as much as I knew I could never trust him, it was better having people I knew here than having no one. I could trust Trang, in a way, but he wouldn't be much help—he never was.

"What's Trang doing here?" I asked Fleck. "I'm not surprised they caught up with you, but why him? Did you kill him or something?"

Before he had a chance to answer me, a limping, reeking man clutching a falling-apart briefcase pushed through us. "Don't just stand there getting in every-body's way!" he whined at us, taking a moment to look us up and down. He had only one eye. Where the other one used to be was a gaping, festering hole, crawling with maggots. "You look new. Shouldn't be down this deep yet. Must have done something *really* rotten."

"What do you mean—" I started to say.

"No time, no time," he said, limping away with his briefcase, immediately lost in the crowd of other people clutching at papers, or holding cardboard folders containing papers. Even the crawling ones had official-looking papers with them, dragging them through the filth, which was suddenly steam-ing, bubbling hot.

We stood farther apart, to get out of peoples' way—but not far enough to get separated from each other, which would have been really easy. "So why Trang?" I asked again, sweat breaking out on my forehead in the heat.

"Haven't you noticed?" Fleck said with difficulty, still having trouble breathing because of the shock of being back here. "The people who run this place are slobs—there aren't any toilets, for example. And so when they zapped me back they weren't precise about it. I was in the car with Trang, and they made a beentsy little mistake and brought him along, too. Happens all the time."

"But where are the cops—or whoever is in charge here?" I asked him. "They brought you back. Shouldn't they be here to meet you—and punish you for running away? And then they'd realize they made a mistake and let him go."

He shrugged hopelessly, paler than ever. "I told you!" he snapped at me, finally getting his breath back. He wiped sweat out of his eyes. "They're slobs. They'll have to find us, and when they do, they're not going to be easy on me. And as for letting Trang out of here." He shook his head back and forth and almost did manage a chuckle.

It was hard getting used to his new, handsome, healthy appearance. It was especially striking because everybody else here—except us—looked the way he used to look. But his voice was the same.

"I thought you said you didn't go here if the crime you committed was to help somebody," I told him, suddenly feeling enraged. "Was that just another lie you fed me?"

He smiled his crafty smile. "Was helping Jen the *only* reason you killed Rusty?" he asked me. "Or might there have been another little motive, too? Envy? Jealousy, perhaps?"

I lost control. "I never would have known him if you hadn't set the whole thing up!" I screamed at him. "And I wasn't planning to kill him—it was an accident. It was the same as if you did it yourself! You knew what he was like!" I started punching him. He kneed me in the groin and I staggered away, slipping and almost falling on the ice, trying not to touch it with my wounded hand. The temperature kept fluctuating instantly between too hot and too cold. You never had a chance to get used to one or the other.

"No point in fighting with each other down here," Fleck said, shivering. "There's plenty of worse things to fight than me. You'll find out soon enough."

A new karaoke song came blasting on, "Singin' in the Rain," horribly wavering and out of tune, the singers still laughing in an unbearably irritating way. Heavy snow began pouring down on us.

I put my hands over my head, trying to keep my teeth from chattering. The prison uniform was very thin. It was hard getting used to the fact that I was going to be here for eternity. Eternity? I couldn't imagine it. But it had to be even worse for Trang. "Can't we find somebody important and tell them he's not even *dead* yet? Can't they tell?"

Now Fleck laughed for real. But even though he laughed, even though he looked better than I had ever seen him, he was like a different person here, stooped and cringing. "You think they care? If he wanted to get out that way, he'd have to spend the next twenty years filling out papers in order to prove he's alive, and didn't commit a damnable act. That's why everybody's running around. To fill out papers, and then push through crowds around the officials—no orderly lines here—to give them the papers and get them stamped, in hopes of avoiding worse torture. Or to buy favors or get something to eat, paying with more torture." He shrugged again. "And then the papers never get approved anyway. They're always missing one little necessary thing."

"What am I going to do then?" Trang's voice was so hushed with fear that we could barely hear him in all the racket.

For some reason I cared about Trang. It was a way of avoiding trying to imagine eternity here. "Can't we even *try* to help him?" I asked.

Fleck looked around, checking on his bearings again. "Okay, we can try." He shrugged. "Hell, we can *all* try to get out. But the chance of it working *without* filling out papers and waiting in crowds for twenty years is about one in a billion. And whatever you do, don't get separated from me or you'll never get out of here. We better hold hands. It's easy to get lost in the crowd here. Happens to everybody all the time."

Fleck took Trang's hand, I was glad to see. I grabbed Trang's hand, Fleck pulling us along through the snow. Was it possible that Fleck could get us all out? He had done it once. Following him—and especially not losing him—was our only hope.

We wove our way through the crowds of emaciated, maimed people holding papers, hurrying and limping helter-skelter. I knew I was squeezing Trang's hand very tightly. I hoped Trang was holding just as tightly to Fleck—the only one of us who knew his way around here.

I could feel the phone weighing in my pocket. Unfortunately, the pocket was small, and the shape of the phone—and the part of the battery peeking out—was very easy to see. Still, I was lucky the prison uniform *had* a pocket. If it didn't, somebody would be more likely to take the phone away from me—that was just the kind of thing that would happen here. I kept checking other people, and no one else had a cell phone. You'd think people who died in car crashes because they were talking on the phone while driving would have had their phones in hell, but they must have all dropped them at the moment of death. I had been too paralyzed from the lethal injection to drop mine.

We passed something like a restaurant, except there were no tables, just a skeletal withered creature behind a food stall in a filthy apron dishing out some kind of slop to the hungry crowd around it. Only those with certain tickets could get fed—how long had they worked and been tortured to get their tickets? The bowls were dirty, light-blue plastic, and leaky.

The food was a thin brown liquid with slimy things like pieces of fat floating in it. Wormlike animals squirmed around in the warm broth, which was steaming in the cold. The smell was so disgusting—like rotting garbage in a human sewer—that I couldn't imagine eating it. I tried not to breathe as we passed by it. But what if I was starving, like all the people here? If I was going to be here for eternity I'd have to get hungry some day.

There it was again: Eternity. I pushed the thought out of my mind. Thinking about it made me want to kill myself. But how could I kill myself when I was already dead? Death was not an escape from here. There was no escape. And it was all Fleck's fault.

Stop thinking about it! I screamed inwardly.

We came to the tallest building yet, so tall it disappeared into the cloudy sky. Fleck was heading for it. Just as we reached it, an old metal cage of an elevator on the outside of the building came creaking down, and landed on ground level with a jolt that made everybody inside it stagger—though they couldn't stagger much since they were so tightly pressed against each other. They started pouring out, right beside us.

"No, don't even *think* of riding in those things,"

Fleck said, pulling us past it. "They crash all the time. And if you're inside one when it does, you don't die, of course, you just get *more* maimed. They never stop on the right floor. The dopes inside haven't learned that yet. Anyway, this one only goes down. You can't get in that way. This way."

And I saw there was a deep pit underneath where the elevator was hanging. It was only going further down. People still crowded into it.

Fleck pulled us around to another side of the building, constantly weaving and pushing through the milling, stinking crowds. Some of them were naked, some had on underwear, others tried to cover themselves with rags. It was easy to see that many of the people had sores worse than Fleck had ever had, their entire bodies covered with wounds and blisters and disgusting oozing rashes.

On this side of the building was an entrance, uneven and crumbling, like it had been blasted open. Creatures stood on either side of the entrance, guarding it. The sight of them made me want to scream out loud.

The two guards were humanoid, but definitely not human. Their flat heads looked like they'd been squashed in a vise, making their eyes into slits and stretching out all their features like something in a funhouse mirror. They each had four arms and big bellies. The lower pair of arms and hands were strong and powerful, the upper pair much smaller, like the tiny arms on a T. rex. They wore only loincloths, which looked sticky with bodily fluids and excretions. Except for on their powerful lower arms, their red scaly skin hung off their torsos in folds. Each held thick barbed whips in two of its four gloved hands, passing them from hand to hand depending on where people were trying to get in.

Of course there was a big crowd around the entrance, pushing, but the squashed-headed guards kept whipping the people to make them go away.

"Hold on tight," Fleck said, and we all gripped our hands even more tightly as he very cleverly worked his way through the crowd, pushing ahead of people right and left, kicking gently—he was adept at this, probably because he'd had a lot of practice. It was surprisingly easy for us to push through the crowd, but then I realized it was because we just got here, and were stronger than the other people, who had been starved and tortured for years. I kept feeling like saying "Excuse me" when we pushed ahead of someone or I stepped on somebody's toes or hooves, but it seemed pointless. Their response was to kick and scream at us, and try to pull us apart, but they were too weak to have much effect. We clung together more tightly than ever.

Sooner than I expected we were at the front of the crowd. Fleck pulled us toward the guards, bent over, obsequious. When he got close enough to one of them, it automatically slashed him with its whip—not on his face, luckily, but across the clothed part of his body. But it still hurt, and his sports coat and shirt were torn. He staggered and almost fell. But he didn't back away like other people had.

The other guard spat something red onto the dirt in front of him. "You think we're letting you in here, scum?" he growled at Fleck. "None of you got any papers. Nobody gets in here without papers. Go and get some papers or we'll keep slashing you." He turned to the other guard. "Right, Gack? So if you want to stick around here, prepare for more slashing." They both laughed. Then they passed their whips quickly between their four arms and hands in a threatening way.

"I'm helping this man." Fleck gestured at Trang. "He doesn't have any papers because he came here by accident," he continued—it was the first time I'd ever heard him sound timid. "He's not dead; he hasn't committed any sins. I think in here is the only place he can get the papers he needs."

"Helping? *Helping?*" the creature roared at him. "What does that mean, 'helping'?" He said the word in a nasty, sarcastic falsetto. "Helping doesn't happen around here. Who cares whether they're alive or dead, or here by accident? Desert them and leave them to fend for themselves. You might earn some points for doing that." The guards laughed again.

Fleck stood up a little straighter. "Maybe I could earn even more points another way," he said, lifting his free hand in an attempt to appear jaunty. "What if I took them to the special torture chamber on level 283? Then they'd get tortured for no reason at all. Wouldn't you like that? Wouldn't *that* earn me five points and ten bonus points?"

The two guards looked at each other again, wondering if they could believe him or not. Fleck had said several times that they weren't too bright in hell. I hoped they wouldn't notice the object in my back pocket. I was sure they'd take the phone away from me if they saw it. And for some reason I didn't really understand it seemed terribly important to me to keep it.

"Well . . ." the guard who had whipped Fleck said. "If you put that young man with all the hair in the Scavenger's Daughter for seventy-two hours, we might let you have three points and two bonus points."

"How about seven points and three bonus if I permanently cripple both of them?" Fleck bargained.

I wanted to argue at this point, but I kept my mouth shut.

"Five's the max we can give, and two bonus. We'd give you passes for floor 283 only—can't go nowhere else. What you think, Grack?"

The other guard shifted from flat foot to flat foot. I noticed smoke drifting up behind him. Suddenly he brightened, and his four hands began fluttering in the air. "Only if I get to give them the passes!" he said with excitement. "Oh, Gack, let me do it, please!"

"Okay. Give 'em their passes and let 'em in. Nobody will let them nowhere but Torture 283 after that."

Fleck stepped toward the guard with the smoke, holding his free hand out and cringing even more. I wondered why just getting a pass made him cringe.

The guard turned around and stepped to the side and then we saw the fiery brazier behind him, which had a lot of metal rods sticking out of the flames. He held the two whips in his powerful lower arms, and quickly poked through the rods with his smaller, more delicate upper hands. When he found the right rod he pulled it out—a glowing red branding iron. Fleck had known this was going to happen.

The guard pressed the branding iron onto the back of Fleck's hand. There was a sizzling sound. Fleck managed to howl only briefly. I smelled burning flesh. And now burnt into the skin of his hand were the words 283 ONLY.

The other people waiting to get in were milling around us, pushing, trying to get past us to the entrance. In a second we'd be separated—they'd get in between Fleck and Trang and me. And the guards were not interested in protecting us.

We had no choice. Fleck knew the way things worked around here and he'd said this was a slight possibility of getting out. A burn was worth it. And we had to do it before people got ahead of us.

Trang understood that, and presented his hand. He didn't make a sound when he was burned, just closed his eyes and gritted his teeth. It made me think he had been through things like this before, maybe in his own country.

I held out my left hand, the one with the punctured wrist from all the painful IV attempts at my execution; they had finally stopped bleeding. I figured this side of me was already damaged. I was sweating and breathing hard. When the creature stuck the thing against my skin it hurt like crazy, and I yelled. And it kept on hurting, even after he took the brand away.

"Awright, get inside," one of the guards said, dangerously flicking his whip right next to my face. "And don't think you can get nowhere but Torture 283." The three of us took hands now flaming with pain and ran inside.

"Hey, what's that thing you got in your pocket?" one of the guards bellowed. "Get back and hand it over now!" I looked behind, the guard was starting toward us. Then he stepped back, reluctant to leave his post—if he did, he would obviously get punished. He also had to keep whipping the people trying to get in. "I'm telling all the other guards you got something!" he yelled after us, putting a big, clunky object to his ear.

Another elevator, inside, on the opposite wall from the outside one, plummeted down and crashed. The building shook. The people inside tumbled all over each other, and there were screams and a sound that could only be the crunching of bones. When the doors opened, some of the people inside literally had to slither their way out; their legs had become useless. And still, more people were waiting to shove their way inside.

Rusty, in his once beautiful but now stained and tattered clothes, emerged from the crowd. The clothes hung loosely on him. He had lost all his muscles and was skinnier than I was now, from being starved. He spotted us instantly and started quickly in our direction.

It was a shock to see him, though now I realized I should have expected it. "Run!" I said to Fleck. "I can't stand this. I don't want to face him!"

Rusty had died months ago, and must be getting used to the way things worked here. The wound in his head had stopped bleeding, but it hadn't closed or healed over, probably because he was dead. A good quarter of the bone of his skull was missing, with tatters of skin hanging down around it. His brain seemed to have swollen, as if released from bondage, and bulged out from the huge hole in his skull. The wound had also twisted up one of his eyes and half his mouth, which seemed to be paralyzed, fixed in a half smile. He was as hideously grotesque as anything

I had seen here yet—especially with the fragment that remained of the lock of red hair hanging over his forehead. I remembered how proud of his looks he had been.

He was getting closer, clutching some papers. Fleck and Trang seemed rooted in place.

"Hurry!" I begged Fleck. "We've got to get away from him!"

"You can't stand to face what you yourself did, and the reason you're here?" Fleck asked me sardonically, still not moving.

"I didn't mean to do it! It's all your fault it happened!" I would have run away from Rusty by myself, but I didn't dare leave Fleck—I had no idea how to get to the place he was taking us, which might be an escape.

And by now Rusty had reached us. He was trying to grin at us, the unparalyzed half of his mouth twisted upward. It only made him look more horrifying. "Well, well, I've been expecting you," he said, and the words came out like mush because of his ruined mouth, hard to understand. He looked me up and down. "You're a mess," he had the nerve to say, managing to sound almost triumphant. "You must have been in jail. It had to be Jen who betrayed you."

He chuckled. "One of the other inmates kill you, or what?"

"Death by lethal injection," Fleck said. "Doesn't that warm your heart, Rusty?"

Rusty made a gurgling sound that must have been a laugh. "Serves him right. He was so skinny before, I didn't believe he could get any skinnier and weaker looking. But he did." Then he noticed my hand. "Level 283?" His eyes lit up. "That's torture, isn't it? Where they use the Scavenger's Daughter. Perfect! And you have to ride the elevator to get there." He made his wet gulping laugh again.

As the elevator slowly began grinding its way up, Fleck leaned close to us and said in a hushed voice, "We're not going there, we're not going to the regular torture rooms. We're going to try another place. Like I said, the chance of it working is a billion to one. But that's better than just giving up."

The karaoke singers were now doing their warped rendition of "Don't Worry, Be Happy." Suddenly they were interrupted by a blaring, echoing announcement. "Keep your eyes out for a long-haired guy with something in his pocket. He's with a live Asian one and a dark-haired cool creep. *We want the thing in his pocket.*"

Now the guards would be looking for us, on top of everything else.

"Don't Worry, Be Happy" came drunkenly back on, filled with stupid laughter.

"You're going to another place?" Rusty said, leaning excitedly toward Fleck—so excited that he made no comment on the announcement. "What do you mean by the chance of it working? You did get out once—you were at my house when he killed me."

"Don't—" I started to say, then stopped myself, not wanting to be too obvious. But if we were trying to get out, the last person I wanted coming with us was Rusty.

"You're the expert, Fleck," Rusty said. "Been here for eight years already. You must know something I don't know."

Now Fleck looked confused. Why hadn't he known that Rusty would want to horn in on where we were going? Why hadn't he tried to get away from him, like I wanted to do? Now it was probably too late to shake him off.

And, in his usual perverse way, Fleck didn't seem to *want* to shake him off. "Like I said, the chance of it working is a billion to one. If you want to try, take hands."

Trang took Fleck's hand again, I took Trang's, and, to my disgust, Rusty grabbed mine. It was my bad hand. His grip was strong, and I cringed away in pain. But I could *feel* that nothing would make him let go. Rusty with his smashed-in head and his brain oozing out and dripping onto the floor.

Fleck, even more quickly now, led us to a crowded wooden stairway opposite the entrance and pulled us onto it. I looked up. The top of the stairway was so far away I couldn't see it through the stinking polluted atmosphere inside the building. And of course the stairway was cheaply made, and some of the steps were actually missing, and we had to take giant steps to get to the next one. The whole thing felt as if it could collapse in a minute—and there were plenty of other people on it, too. They were going down and going up on both sides, so we kept bumping into them or else having to wait for them to squeeze past. Everybody was sweating in the unbearable heat.

As we got higher, Trang got paler. "I . . . I don't know if I can do this, go more higher than this," he said to Fleck. "Being high up in the air—it is something I am very afraid of." He had been so stoic about the burn, but he was afraid of heights.

"Only one more flight," Fleck told him, panting.

"Tell the chink to hurry up!" Rusty yelled.

Fleck pulled us higher. And then Trang, in his efforts not to look down, didn't notice a missing step, and put his foot down into empty space. He screamed as he started to fall. Fleck and I almost fell down with him, but we managed to grab onto the railing and tugged him, hard, and he just barely got his foot up through the empty space and onto the next step. I could feel his hand trembling in mine.

"Hurry up!" "Quit stalling!" "What's the delay there?" people called angrily from above and below us.

The next floor was four. This was the one Fleck wanted; he led us away from the staircase, onto the safer cement. Although maybe it wasn't that much safer. The cement was full of holes and big cracks. They had built this structure as cheaply as possible. So what if a floor or ceiling caved in?

And it was still very crowded here, people hurrying around in any way they could, sweating in the unbearable heat, holding papers, peeking into doorways, looking for the right place to go. There were a lot of doors and they were not arranged in sequence—room 41A was right next to room 49Y. How could you ever get to the right place in here?

Fleck seemed to know. The corridors were a

labyrinth crowded with maimed and sick people, and some things that didn't look like people, but Fleck pulled us unhesitatingly from one corridor to another, never pausing to wonder which way to go, as most other people did.

"How do you know where you're going?" I asked him.

"I've been to this room many, many times. This is where I used the phone. I lucked out. There's a woman in the office we're heading for who especially likes to torture me—don't ask me why. I just let her do it and then she grants me a favor. I hope we can get to her. Maybe she'll help us if she can torture somebody. And she doesn't have a Scavenger's Daughter. Sometimes her office is really crowded, though. Look out!"

Two four-handed guards were coming by, on the lookout for us maybe, to take the phone away from me. Fleck pulled us out of the way behind another crowd before they saw us.

"What is . . . what is Scavenger's Daughter?" Trang asked. That was the thing Fleck had promised the guards he would use on Trang and me.

Rusty laughed again. It sounded like bubbling mud.

"It's a medieval thing." Fleck paused. "The inquisitors

were very clever about torture. They lock you into the Scavenger's Daughter, including your face, and in only a few days it permanently deforms you. Must hurt like hell." He pointed. "There. That person was in one."

Trang and I glanced over at a crablike thing painfully dragging its way across the floor. You could tell it had been a person, once, but now its limbs and face were impossibly twisted, teeth and limbs sticking out everywhere, like someone born with every genetic deformity there was. I looked quickly away.

All the offices we passed were packed with emaciated people. Inside each office was a counter, and creatures behind it sort of like the guards, but less squat, more businesslike. You could see that they read people's papers really, really slowly and thoroughly, holding them with their small upper hands. And of course there were no lines, just a throng of people pushing and trampling each other to get to the counter whenever somebody got rejected, and sadly stepped away from it.

"We're almost there," Fleck said. "Just around this corner. 45X."

We turned the corner. And there was the doorway

marked 45X. And on it was a sign that read OUT TO LUNCH—FOREVER.

Fleck's shoulders slumped. He just stood there silently, looking more miserable than I'd ever seen him.

"What happened? Where is this woman who helped you?" I asked him.

"Yeah. What's going on?" Rusty wanted to know, scratching the wet exposed part of his brain, which I saw was now crusted by some kind of orange fungus.

Fleck sighed. "My one hope. And she must have gotten canned. She liked to torture certain kinds of people too much, and was giving them too many favors, that must be what happened to her. So they got rid of her. They're probably still getting rid of her. When they do it, they do it very, very slowly."

That made me think of my own death by "humane" lethal injection.

"So what we going to do?" Trang asked, as we stepped back against a wall to get out of the way of the lost people hurrying around, trying to find hopeless offices, shivering in the freezing cold. People fell; the floor was slippery with ice.

"If you want to fill out forms and applications and fight the crowds for twenty years, you better get started," Fleck said. "Before your fingers get frost-bitten and fall off. It happens."

We just stood there bewildered, not knowing what to do. I looked away from the crowds of sickening people and other creatures limping and crawling and squishing all around us with their only hope, their useless papers; these were the people I would be with forever—all because of Fleck and Lola and Rusty and the phone. It didn't bear thinking about.

The phone.

I didn't care about Rusty anymore. I just wanted to get out. "What about the phone?" I said to Fleck. "That's what you used to get out of here the first time."

"Yeah. I was calling to your phone when it was up on *earth.*" He said it like I was an idiot. "When it's down here it's completely different."

"How do you know?" I asked him. "You never had it when you were down here before."

He gave me a funny look.

"Why do the guards want to get it away from me?"

"They just want it because they don't like anybody to have anything special."

"What phone?" Rusty wanted to know. "What are you talking about? Getting out? If we do, I'll get Jen away from you for good this time." Snot drooled out of his mouth.

I ignored him. "But the phone might be different down here," I said to Fleck, beginning to hope. "Maybe there's a *reason* they made that announcement to take it away from me. And there was a game on it that I played. You were walking up a tunnel to the earth. And all you had to do was not look back in order to get out. Up on earth it was just a game. But down here . . . down here, maybe it would be *real.* After all, the game section is called **GAMES FROM REAL HELL**. Maybe down here it really *could* happen!" I was so excited now that I pulled the phone out of my pocket. "Just let me try. We should hold hands again and—"

Fleck pulled the phone away from me. "If anybody does anything with this phone, it's gonna be *me*," he said.

"But it's my phone!" I shouted at him. I hated not having it. "I did it before, I can get to it really fast, and you don't even—"

He pushed me away, stubborn as usual; getting his own way, as usual. Still, using the phone had been *my* idea. "You said it was under **GAMES FROM REAL HELL**?" he asked me.

"Yeah. You push the big key down on the left side, and then scroll down with the upper right key." I grabbed Trang's hand again. "Trang, take Fleck's arm. Be sure you're holding onto him somehow." Trang took hold of Fleck's elbow as he punched the keys. Rusty grabbed my bad hand again, squeezing it too hard again, and I winced.

Around the corner came two tiny-brained, lumbering guards, ignoring all the other people, obviously looking for someone in particular. "Hurry!" I urged Fleck.

"Got the games," he said. "What next?"

"Go to 'Attempts to Escape' and select 'Don't Look Back.' Hurry!" I said again, as the guards with flattened-down faces approached.

"Hey, what's that thing there?" one of the guards said, his long mouth moving like a fish's mouth as he spoke. "You're the guy with long hair they were talking about. You heard the announcement. You can't have no thing like that in here. Gimme it! I said Gimme it! *NOW!*" The guard reached his hand out for the phone. The other one lifted his whips.

Fleck pressed a key.

The guards vanished, the building vanished. We were standing in a dark tunnel, and far, far above us was the starry sky. It was the same tunnel as the game, except that it was night outside now.

And this time it wasn't just a display. This time it was all around us. Real.

16

"Don't look back!" I shouted. "No matter what happens, what you see or hear, don't look behind you. Just keep looking ahead!"

"Don't tell me what to do!" Rusty whined in his garbled voice. But he didn't let go of my hand, and he didn't look back.

Holding hands, we started up the tunnel. It was steep, it was dark, and the ground was uneven. All of us kept stumbling. Fleck was in the lead, holding the phone. I hated it that he had the phone. But at least he had gotten us to the right place. "Just keep looking at the stars!" I said.

A table with four places set on it, and in the middle of it a sizzling hot turkey, floated past. It smelled wonderful, the best ever. Fleck and Trang and I were not hungry, so we weren't tempted. But Rusty, who was beside me, and whose face I could see without looking back, had an expression of longing on his twisted features. He had been in hell for months. He was so thin already. He was starving. He pressed his lips together and forced himself to look away from the turkey.

The starry opening above got a little closer.

A necklace that looked like real diamonds floated past. It would have made a nice present for Mom—she could sell it and get a lot of money. But that didn't matter now. Trang could have used the money, too, but he didn't look back either. Rusty wasn't tempted; he could just buy a necklace like that.

And then there were thudding footsteps behind us, so heavy the ground shook, and snarling. Very deep, wet snarling. It sounded like a pack of big animals—or monsters—following us. They yelped and then roared, getting closer. They smelled like they'd been rolling in other dead animals. This was the hardest one yet. When you think something's following you, it's like an instinct to look back. I had to force my head from turning. "Don't look!" I shouted. "They're not real."

But here, maybe they *were* real.

Still, we all kept looking ahead as the animals got

closer. They were about to reach us. They roared, they thundered, I could feel their hot breath stinking like vomit. The urge to turn back was overwhelming. But I fought it. I didn't turn. Neither did the others.

The animal sounds stopped.

The stars were getting closer. Could this possibly work—a real way out of there? I began to hope even more. "See? Those animals were fake," I said to the others. "Learn from that. Don't pay attention no matter what—"

Hailstones came pelting down on us. *They* sure seemed real—we could really feel them stinging us painfully as they hit our faces and bodies. We kept plodding upward—though Fleck was going a lot slower now. The hailstones were a miserable impediment.

"Nick, Nick, it's Jen," called a voice from behind us that sounded exactly like Jen's. "Please. I'll never get out of here if you don't help me. Please come back for me. I need your help. They got me through the phone. Nick, Nick!"

"Ignore that voice!" I shouted to myself. "*You're* the one who'll never get out if you turn and look!" But I wanted to see her so much. Only for a second. Would one second be too long?

"You're not going to help her?" Rusty asked me,

sounding serious. "How come you're so selfish? All you care about is yourself!"

I wanted to let go of his hand and push him back.

"Oh, Nick, I miss you so much!" Jen cried out. "Please, please! Nothing will be worth it if you don't come back and help me!"

I could hardly stand it. Seeing her face, after what I had been through, would be so wonderful. Could I get away with half a second? And how had they known my name was Nick, or what Jen's voice sounded like?

And then I remembered seeing Jen's face on the cell phone display when I was playing this game, and looking back, and losing. Fleck had said they weren't too bright down here, but there were some things they seemed to be really clever about. It wasn't going to get easier.

"Oh, Nick, what you did wasn't worth anything if you don't help me now!"

What I did. Fleck had said, in his usual taunting way, that killing Rusty had been motivated by jealousy and envy. Okay, maybe they were part of it. But not the main part. I did it for Jen, as much as she hated it. I really believed Rusty would hurt her. I didn't know if she knew that or not.

"*I'm* going to help her if you don't!" Rusty said.

"Go ahead! Go back and help her!" I yelled at him.

But now I knew I had to help him, too. I tugged on his hand to keep him moving forward.

"Nick!" Jen's voice was getting fainter. "Nick!" The voice died away. The stars were closer.

Money came fluttering down, looking as though it would land just behind us. I was able to see that they were hundred-dollar bills. Trang and I needed the money desperately. I could easily get enough so I wouldn't have to work anymore. I was tempted to let go of Trang's hand and grab as many as possible out of the air. "They're not real!" I cried out, again for myself as much as the others. "They won't be any good down there."

And still, none of us gave in. The stars were even closer. We might make it.

A beautiful Asian woman appeared, wearing a long, loose white dress, walking toward us from above, down the tunnel. She was staring hard at Trang, smiling. She said something in a foreign language. All I could understand was that she said the word "Trang," over and over again. She stopped beside him. Her face was full of love. She reached out for him tenderly.

Trang said something to her in Vietnamese. He sounded like he was fighting tears. Her smile deepened.

She had to be an image of the wife he had left behind. "She's fake! She's fake! She's not who you think she is!" I screamed at him.

Without looking away from the woman, Trang reached into the pocket of his threadbare jacket and took out a small cassette tape. He thrust it into my hand. "Tape I make when Fleck talk to you on the phone about Lola and killing Rusty," he said.

I felt a peculiar mixture of emotions. But what I did was to scream at him. "You're giving it to me *now? After* they killed me? Why didn't you play it at the trial? Then I might have lived!"

"Fleck and Lola at trial. I too shy . . . cannot play it when they were there. I think your English word . . . don't want to betray."

"But—but—" I sputtered, even as I slipped the cassette into my pants pocket. It was so typical of Trang to make the tape and then *not* bring it out at the trial, because he was afraid of hurting Fleck and Lola's feelings.

"Lola, and killing me?" Rusty muttered, sounding confused. "But—" His voice choked to a stop.

The beautiful woman threw her arms around

Trang. He put his arms around her to kiss her, as she turned so that he faced back.

And then they were both gone.

"No!" Fleck and I wailed at the same time. We stopped briefly. I felt as if a part of my body had been torn away from me. But even though I felt that way, I still didn't look back, and stepped forward and grabbed Fleck's hand. "But it's not *fair!*" I said, close to tears. "Yeah, he was dim. But he was a nice man. He didn't even die. And now . . . now he's stuck there! I can't stand it! It's not fair."

And as I spoke we walked forward. And then I said to myself, "Just keep going. Keep your eyes on the stars."

"Thanks a bunch for getting me outta here, man," Rusty said snidely in his garbled voice.

It was easy to ignore him. The stars were very close now. Only a few more steps and we'd be out of the tunnel. Where would we end up?

And then a shower of filth—excrement and thick bodily fluids—came pounding down on us, pushing us back. We struggled against it, but it got stronger, like police hoses. We could barely see the stars now, there was so much filth shooting down on us. If we turned around it would stop.

We didn't turn around. A few more steps.

The filth dissolved. I was out of the tunnel. Fleck and the phone were gone. Rusty was gone. I was standing alone on a sidewalk.

The sidewalk in front of the police station where they had arrested me.

17

I was dripping stinking shit onto the sidewalk. I walked up the steps to the police station and pushed open the door and went inside, leaving puddles of vomit and excrement everywhere I went. I didn't care.

I wasn't sure exactly how this had happened. Had the phone worked to get me—and not Fleck and Rusty—out of hell because I was the one who legally owned it? Was that enough to make it work?

Or had Fleck been telling the truth about motivation? He had schemed to murder Rusty purely in order to work his way toward getting a fortune—his motivation had been completely selfish. Rusty had murdered Fleck—his motivation had been completely selfish, too. Mine hadn't. Lola and Fleck had influenced me a lot, especially Fleck. But mainly I had done it to save Jen from Rusty. There was no money in it for me.

Did they care in hell? Would they come and find me and bring me back some day, as they had done to Fleck? Somehow I didn't think so. Our situations were so different. Just the fact that they had let me out through the tunnel, and not Fleck or Rusty, made me believe they might leave me alone and not bring me back.

I hoped.

It also seemed right that the phone had gone back to hell with Fleck. That's where it belonged.

It just so happened that the cop on duty at the front desk was the same one who had arrested me. He had also shackled me to the gurney at the execution. It was utter joy to see the expression on his face when I walked up and stood in front of the desk. If this had been a movie with special effects his eyes would have popped a foot out of his head.

He stood up slowly, his palms flat on the desk, his mouth open, his face dead white. He was literally seeing a ghost, a dead man come back to life. It was one of the greatest moments of my life, second only to meeting Jen and having her like me as much as I liked her.

"Sorry about all this," I said, running my hand across the desk and leaving a trail of unspeakable filth on some official looking papers. "It was kind of dirty where I was, and not so easy getting out. But I made it."

"What . . . ? Are you . . . ? But you can't! Are you a twin?"

"If it makes it easier for you to believe that I'm a twin, then yeah, I'm a twin," I said. "Could I call my mother, please?"

A man who had been lounging in a chair beside the desk, who was not in uniform, jumped up, as the room began filling with more cops. "But that's . . . he looks exactly like Nick Gordon, the boy who was just executed for murder," the man said. He whipped out a camera and took a flash picture of me. "I covered that case. Nobody said he had a twin."

"I'm not saying anything yet," I said, enjoying this immensely. "Can I please call my mother? Oh, and I have a tape here that might interest you, but I don't want to touch it until I wash my hands." I shook myself off, watching the shit splatter on the floor. "In fact, if there's a bathroom here it might be nice if I could shower and change. I think everyone would feel a lot better if you let me do that. I must smell pretty bad. I can't tell anymore; I've been like this long enough to get used to the smell."

They let me take a shower and change, and put me in a cell, where I was when Mom got there. She cried and cried and would have hugged me if I hadn't been behind bars. The only explanation they could come up with was that the inexperienced orderly had made a mistake and not given me enough of the drug, and then somehow I had escaped from the morgue. It was full of holes but it was easier for them to believe than the truth.

The tape was great. It was the one thing Trang hadn't messed up, and it made Fleck's and Lola's intentions all too clear. She'd be in trouble now, for corrupting a minor. And now the police understood better how Nick Gordon had been coerced to the breaking point.

They kept me in jail overnight. The next day they summoned Lola to the police station. They let me watch through a one-way mirror as they played the tape to her. There was Fleck's voice, loud and clear, saying, "I'd be killing Rusty to help Lola, to save her. She wants him dead, too."

Lola went ashen, in all her expensive finery.

"What do you know about this?" a state prosecutor asked her.

"It's . . . it's not possible. Fleck died eight years ago." She started crying.

They couldn't hold her on anything; she had no direct connection to Rusty's murder. But if news of the tape ever got out, her reputation—what was left of it—would be ruined.

What to do with me was the real problem. Legally, Nick Gordon had been convicted of murder and executed. There was no way to change that. And they really weren't sure who I was. So they let me finish high school in a special school for problem kids.

Since I was no longer really a criminal, I was legally able to sell the tape to the highest bidder—a tabloid. I made a tremendous amount of money by telling them what hell is like. BOY RETURNS FROM HELL screamed the headline. Of course there was also coverage of the strange case in the regular newspapers and on TV. The world considered me a miracle. I gave most of the money I made to Mom to put away. Now she wouldn't have to work so hard all the time.

It was wonderful in the state school compared to

hell. There were a lot of books, and limited TV, and computers! I did better in school than ever.

And I thought a lot about what I had done, how stupid I had been, how easy it had been to squeeze the trigger and kill Rusty. Too easy. I knew I would never hold another gun.

Because of my miraculous celebrity, all the colleges wanted me. I went to State, because they gave me a total scholarship, including room and board. Jen could have gone anywhere, but she went to State to be with me—we were in the same class now because the trial and imprisonment had put me way behind. Her parents would have liked the prestige of a fancier school, but they couldn't stop her—she just didn't apply anywhere else. Finally she understood better what kind of pressure had been on me. We are closer than ever now.

Lola hadn't done anything actually criminal. But she was shunned. From what I could tell, she was as much of a lonely recluse as when she had been hiding from Rusty. She just had more money. But, because of the money, she still couldn't trust anybody. Was it her the men liked, or her money? There was no way she could ever know.

But I didn't want to think about her. Trang mattered

more. My heart ached for him. He had been spineless, but decent. I kept thinking it just couldn't happen that he could be stuck in hell. What had he really done wrong? Fleck said they made mistakes like that all the time, but how could I believe Fleck?

I thought of calling the cell phone, but I didn't dare. Fleck had been holding it when he got swept back to hell, not Trang. I was sure they had taken the phone away from Fleck, but that didn't mean Trang would have it again. It seemed too dangerous to call a number in hell. There was still a chance they could find me and whisk me back. I would have to live with that forever. That was my real punishment.

But somehow I hoped that the woman who had gone with Trang in the tunnel had not been a fake. I hoped she had really been Trang's wife, and that they were together, somewhere. Jen and I talked about it a lot.

And the more we did, the more I began to believe that Trang was with his loved one, too.

ABOUT THE AUTHOR

WILLIAM SLEATOR

is considered a master of science fiction and thrillers for middle grade readers and young adults. R. L. Stine calls Sleator "one of my favorite young adult writers" and *Publishers Weekly* calls his work "gleefully icky." Sleator divides his time between homes in Boston and rural Thailand.

This book was designed and art directed by Chad W. Beckerman. The text is set in 12-point Adobe Garamond, a typeface that is based on those created in the sixteenth century by Claude Garamond. Garamond modeled his typefaces on those created by Venetian printers at the end of the fifteenth century. The modern version used in this book was designed by Robert Slimbach, who studied Garamond's historic typefaces at the Plantin-Moretus Museum in Antwerp, Belgium. The display type is Felina Gothic.